AMBER'S HEAT

GUARDED SOULS

LEXXIE COUPER

Amber's
HEAT

Guarded Souls Book Three

LEXXIE COUPER

The characters and events portrayed in this book are fictitious. Any similarity to real persons, living or dead, is purely coincidental and not intended by the author.

Amber's Heat
Copyright © 2019 by Lexxie Couper
Editing by Kelli Collins

DEDICATION

For my karate girls: Jackie, Norms and Kelie. For kicking my butt, giving me words of encouragement, and making me believe in myself. Not only in the dojo, but in life.

AMBER'S HEAT

PROLOGUE
TOPANGA CANYON, CALIFORNIA

This is insane.

Crouching lower behind the young manzanita tree, the low, persistent hum of mosquitos buzzing in her ears, Amber squinted into the darkness.

Damn, she should have ask Mick if could've lent her a pair of night-vision goggles. All she could see of the house buried in the forest was a large black shape into which Kitt Newton had disappeared a few moments ago.

Of course, Mick—already suspicious after the whole "can you find anything out about this DNA" situation—would probably have handcuffed her to his weight bench until she gave him so answers, so yeah...*not* asking him for night-vision goggles was probably a sound move.

But still, it would have been nice to actually *see* the man she was...

Stalking? Are we going with that word yet?

No, she *wasn't* stalking. Scientists didn't stalk. Well, none of the scientists she knew did. She was researching. Gathering and collating information, testing hypotheses...

Renting a Prius for silent pursuit, buying camo clothes for easy...err...camouflage, packing telescopic lenses, taking photos...

It sounded a lot like stalking. Good grief, Mick wouldn't just handcuff her to his weight bench if he knew what she was up to, he'd throw her in jail.

But Mick didn't know what *she* knew. Mick didn't know about the evidence she was following. If he did he'd—

One of the side pouches in her camo pants started vibrating. A lot.

"Damn it."

Sinking lower to the pebbly ground, she dug her phone free.

An image of a blond-haired, blue-eyed man in his mid-forties grinned at her from its screen.

Biting back a groan, she connected the call and rammed her phone to her ear. "What?" she ground out. "I'm busy."

"Why did you ask Mick to do a trace on human DNA, sis?"

Damn it. Again. Trust her big brother to blab. To his twin.

"I'm following a trail, Ray," she whispered, peering through the bushes. Nope, so sign of movement. "If it leads to what I think it—"

"Damn it, Amber. You're *not* Indiana Jones."

"Jones was an archeologist."

"Malcom Reynolds, then."

"The captain of the Serenity?"

"The what?"

"The Serenity. Spaceship. Brown coats. Joss Whedon."

"What the..." An exasperated growl came through the phone. "Then who the hell did Jeff Goldblum play in Jurassic Park?"

"Dr. Ian Malcolm. A mathematician."

"No!" More growling. "The other guy. The actor's Australian. Or New Zealand."

"Alan Grant." She took another peek at the house. "You're telling me I'm not Alan Grant. *He* was the paleontologist."

"That's what I'm telling you."

"But I *am* a paleontologist, Ray. So I'm missing your—"

A bright beam of white light cut the night as the front door of the house flung open.

For a split second the silhouette of a tall, hulking man filled the white rectangle, shoulders hunched. And then, as Amber's heart smashed into her throat, he stripped his shirt up over his head and off his six-foot-six foot frame, tossed it aside and positively threw himself into a wild sprint forward.

Straight towards where she crouched in the bushes.

"Shit," she gasped, floundering backward in a wild flail.

Landing on her ass, she bit back a yelp of pain and crunched her body up as small as she could.

Just as a massive shape barged through the undershrub and shrubs, barely a few feet away from her.

Not the *man* Kitt Newton.

Not a man at all.

But a wolf.

An enormous, snarling, dire wolf. A creature extinct for over a ten-thousand years.

Kitt Newton, in his dire wolf form.

And she'd missed the transformation from human to wolf thanks to her over-protective big brother. Damn it.

"Ray," she mumbled, heart racing as she returned her phone to her ear, "I love you, but I've gotta go."

Move over Dr. Grant. She had some chasing to do.

1

W aking up in a silver-barred cage wasn't on Kitt's to-do list.

Although, 'regaining consciousness' would be more accurate. 'Waking up' implied he'd been complicit in his transition from alert to...not alert.

Some unknown son of a bitch had shot him.

But with what?

Exploring the angry wound on his left side with gentle fingers, he bit back a hiss of pain. It wasn't getting better. Wasn't healing.

His dire-wolf *croi* would have healed a normal bullet wound, or knife wound by now. One of the perks of being a shifter—no real need for healthcare. Of course, part of his employment package with Guarded Souls included full healthcare, complete with dental and hospital coverage. He was pretty certain the generous inclusion was Kade's attempt at ironic humor: how many of the non-human team at Guarded Souls would ever *need* full healthcare coverage, given all of them had the ability to heal by non-human means?

The wound in his left side though?

He pushed a little on the raw skin, put a little more pressure on his ribs, and almost broke his molars grinding his teeth at the shard of excoriating pain detonating through his torso and up into his shoulder.

"What did you shoot me with, you prick?" he bellowed into the darkness.

His voice bounced around the silence, and died.

Silence.

Either his capture had left him alone in whatever miserable place the cage was located, or he was enjoying the show without making his presence known.

Apart from that one introductory line—uttered about an hour ago—the hunter hadn't interacted with him at all.

Ah, you're finally conscious, the unseen hunter had murmured from the bowels of the darkness. *Excellent. That makes me very happy. I knew I'd one day catch the last dire wolf in existence, and I hate to think I'd mortally wounded you when I had.*

Kitt lowered his hand from his side and scanned the blackness surrounding him.

No movement. Not even a hint.

Drawing in a deep breath, he tasted the air.

Nope. Nothing.

The only scent flowing through his nose belonged to old dirt and grim and what could be moldy paper. Wherever he was, it once housed engines of some kind, and possibly a lot of paper.

Printing factory, maybe?

"What's the chance you're going to show yourself any time soon?" he yelled.

His questions echoed around the black emptiness and faded away.

"Didn't think so," he muttered, lowering himself to the cage's floor.

Pain ricocheted up his side and into his shoulder again, and he winced.

What had the hunter shot him with? His body had ways of dealing with the normal threat to his supernatural genetics. The one time he'd been shot with a silver bullet, his body had taken less than thirty minutes to work the bullet out.

Yeah, he'd been weak and feverish for an hour or so after, but he'd recovered quickly.

This...

Sit still. Breathe. Slow your heart. Wait.

Wait. The only thing he could do. Someone at Guarded Souls would notice his absence and track him down. Hell, all James had to do was close his eyes and think of a person and he'd locate him.

But the last you heard, the psychotic sorcerer still had James. And you wolfed out on Nim halfway through your phone call with her. She probably thinks you're still running wild somewhere up in the Topanga Canyon hills.

Grinding his teeth again, he glared at the darkness enveloping him.

Can't see a fucking...

He blinked, an icy finger tracing up his spine. He *couldn't* see a thing. He should be able to. Even when in human form, his vision was preternatural, as heightened as that of his dire wolf form. And a dire wolf—like most animals of the canine species, even those species alive today—saw better at night than in the day.

"You've just realized you can't see the way you're meant to," a disembodied voice floated from beyond the cage's bars. "Am I correct?"

Kitt's hackles prickled at the smug joy in the hunter's voice. His inner wolf growled.

"Have you also noticed," the voice continued, "you haven't shifted form yet? Or even attempted to?"

The icy finger clawed over Kitt's scalp. He stiffened, his throat tightening.

The prick was right. He hadn't.

Why not?

Pulling another deep breath, he released the restraint he held—almost constantly—on his *croi*, the ancient magic the governed his human/dire wolf forms.

Nothing.

No quickening of his blood, no rippling of his flesh into fur. No tearing of bone and muscle...

Nothing.

"You see?" the hunter's voice floated on the darkness. "Effective, yes?"

"What have you done to me?" Kitt snarled, leaping to his feet.

Agony erupted in his side and his knees crumpled. He slammed his knuckles to the floor, halting his fall. But only just.

A low laugh reverberated through the air. "A concoction of my own making. It retards the transformation process a being like yourself goes through. While it's in your system, you're trapped in human form. Much like you're trapped in a cage now. Clever, yes?"

"*Your* making?" Kitt slowly turned, trying to pinpoint the hunter's location.

Another laugh. "I'm not just a pretty face. Although, you can't see that, can you? Not until I turn on the lights."

A sharp double clap cracked the silence, and the room flooded with light.

"Clappers are a wonderful invention, aren't they?" the tall, slender man standing three feet on the other side of the cage's bars said. A smile stretched his thin lips as he looked at Kitt, awakening more creases in his wrinkled face. Delight danced in his blue eyes. "Now you see me..." he raised his gnarled hands beside his long, narrow head, and clapped twice.

Light vanished.

"Now you don't," he finished.

Kitt lunged at the bars, and howled as pain tore through him. Up his side, into his shoulder, up his neck.

He crunched to the floor, shoulders hunched, head low. God, was this what true human pain felt like? This tearing, burning hell?

Planting his palms on the grimy concrete beneath him, he pushed himself back upright...and fell again as a coughing fit attacked him.

Cough after violent cough, as if his throat was trying to rip and hammer from his body. Coughs that clenched his gut and bowed his spine. Followed by the distinct tang of copper on the air and the sensation of moisture on his lips and chin.

Blood. He was coughing up blood.

Fuck, he was coughing up—

Another double clap filled the air, and white light destroyed the blackness. "Oh, that doesn't look good."

"Wh-what did you...shoot me with?" Kitt wiped at his mouth, the ting of his own blood biting into his sinuses. Lifting his head, he glared at the elderly man—now standing a foot farther back from the bars.

The hunter smiled. Preened. More wrinkles seamed his leathery face. Just how old was he? At least sixty? Maybe? "Hollow-tip silver bullet, filled with ground dragon bone, plus a little...secret ingredient, and coated in the very compound preventing you from shifting. Again, my own design. My skills are quite sought after among some of my fellow guild members."

Guild members?

Kitt's breath caught in his blood-lined throat. The pain in his side and shoulder flared hotter. Biting back a groan, he met the hunter's stare. "You're a member of the *Monstrum Venator* guild?"

The hunter's smile stretched into a wide grin and he dipped his head in a small acknowledgement. "I am. The one with the most trophies, you'll be happy to know. Or maybe not, given your..." He waved a hand at the cage. "...current situation."

Fuck.

Kitt narrowed his eyes and took a step closer to the bars. The hunter hurried a step back. Good. "If you planned to kill me when you shot me, I'd be dead now. So you have other plans. What are they? The *Monstrum Venator* aren't known for their subtly. Or compassion."

"Ah, you know of us then."

"I've tangled with your kind before."

Briefly. Three hundred years ago.

An altercation with a member of the guild of hunters who targeted non-human beings had brought Kitt and Kade, the now-owner of Guarded Souls Protection and Security together. The *Monstrum Venator* had the vampire bound to a massive crucifixion cross in the middle of a dense track of tropical forest in what would become known as the Olympic Peninsular in Seattle, and was about to sink a silver stake into his chest when Kitt burst into the clearing...running from a predator of an entirely different kind: a mamma grizzly bear intent on eating him.

Kitt had taken care of the surprised and unprepared hunter in a heartbeat, and the grizzly had decided the freshly killed *Monstrum Venator* was a better meal to be had than a running dire wolf.

Kade swore a life-debt to Kitt on the spot. Kitt was happy with just a job. He'd been working for the formidable, mysterious vampire in one capacity or another since. Guarded Souls was just the latest incarnation of their arrangement.

"Ah, I see." The hunter pursed his lips, running a slow gaze over Kitt. "And you lived? Huh. That's surprising."

Kitt bared his canines in a toothy smile. "Don't believe your guild's own recruiting propaganda. You're the first living *Monstrum Venator* I've seen for many years. And I know of quite a few of my fellow non-humans who've encountered members of your guild. Ask me how many *Monstrum Venator* survived those encounters?"

A muscle twitched above the hunter's watery right eye.

Kitt took another step closer to the bars, braced himself, and wrapped his fingers around their cold silver length.

Searing white-hot pain lanced through his palms and up his arms. Sinking into his chest and gut.

He gripped the bars tighter, refusing to crumple in agony, and locked his stare on the hunter. "Go on," he growled. "Ask me."

Blue eyes regarded him, guarded. Wary. "I think I liked you more when you were unconscious, wolf."

Kitt flashed his canines again, even as his mind screamed in protest at the pain consuming him, threatening to overwhelm him—like boiling acid and frozen steel sinking into his skin and muscles. "Bitten off more than you can chew, old man?"

The hunter remained motionless. The tick above his eye twitched.

"I can smell your sweat," Kitt said. If he didn't let go of the bars soon, he'd pass-out. "And your fear."

The tick twitched again.

Kitt ground his teeth, unblinking. Unblinking...

And then, with a strangled growl, yanked his hands free of the bars and stumbled backward, black swirls of pain fogging his vision, the wound in his side an inferno of grief and agony.

The hunter's eyebrows shot up. His eyes widened, and he laughed, the sound smug and triumphant. "Impressive." He laughed again, shaking his head and stabbing a finger at Kitt. "You almost had me fooled. Oh, I'm very glad I didn't kill you. I can't wait to show you to Xi."

Snarl tearing from his throat, Kitt threw himself at the bars.

The hunter screamed, scrambling backward.

Slumping to his knees, giddy and weak, Kitt let out a low chuckle. "Chicken."

Chest heaving, the hunter smoothed down his shirt front and then his wispy silver hair. "You *are* entertaining. I wasn't expecting that. Your kind don't usually offer such fun."

Kitt stiffened. Pain wracked his body. His inner wolf—trapped and impotent—snarled again. "My kind?"

Dire wolf shifter? *He* was the last dire wolf shifter. Had been for over two centuries, and unless the skinny *Monstrum Venator* had access to a fountain of youth—something Nim swore existed and she was one day going to locate—there was no way the hunter was responsible for the second last dire wolf shifter's death.

Basia.

A cold finger traced up Kitt's bowed spine at the name. Basia had been the last female dire wolf shifter alive. They'd circled each other for almost fifty years, duty to their species demanding they mate, an intense dislike for each other keeping them apart.

Dire wolves mated for life.

The night Kitt had decided he and Basia should put aside their differences and do what had to be done, Basia turned up dead. He'd attempted to find her killer. He'd failed.

Guilt still ate him every damn hour. If he hadn't been so stubborn, she would have been with him and she wouldn't have—

"Monsters," the hunter sneered, stepping closer to the cage. "Unnatural creatures."

"Ah." Kitt swallowed. Unlike the pain from holding the silver bars, the pain in his side hadn't faded. "*My* kind." He caught the man's stare with his own and held it. "The kind *your* kind hunt. Have you heard of deer? No real threat to your existence when you hunt deer, and all you need is a permit and a rifle. Not a...whatever the hell you shot me with."

The hunter smirked. "Where's the fun in hunting something that doesn't have the ability to kill you?"

"Grizzle bear then."

"Bears don't threaten the natural order of the world, Mr. Newton. Your kind do."

"So you hunt non-humans to save the world?"

"It's the reason I joined the guild." The smirk stretched wider. "Of course, now I do it for the sport. And the bragging rights."

Kitt's wolf's hackles rose. "Bragging rights?"

"Yes. A fellow guild member and I are embroiled in a

long and thoroughly enjoyable competition to see who captures and kills the most remarkable game."

Scrubbing at his face, Kitt growled again. "I am going to rip your throat out."

The hunter laughed. "No, you're going to stay in the cage. And I'm going to go have dinner." He raised his hands to the right side of his head. "See you soon."

He clapped twice, and the area plunged into blackness again.

Closing his eyes, Kitt drew a slow breath. Fire erupted in his side, lashing up into his shoulder.

He bit back a wince, and pressed his hand to his ribs. Still wet with blood.

Would he start healing when the concoction the hunter shot him with left his system? Or had the bastard injected it in *after* shooting him?

Pulling another slow breath, he tuned his focus into his wolf.

The savage, canine side of his duel spirit snarled within, agitated.

But there. Not silenced, just...hobbled.

Exhaling, Kitt relaxed the tenuous, mystical hold he kept on his human form. Waited for the prickling sensation over his skin and limbs to begin—the precursor to the shift into wolf form.

It didn't. Instead, his side erupted in fresh fire and pain.

"Damn it," he muttered, opening his eyes. What did he do?

He squinted into the dark, trying to discern anything apart from the faint outline of the silver bars caging him.

Shot or not, he'd be able to physically overwhelm the hunter in a straight-up man-to-man fight—the prick was reed-thin and looked fragile with age, but what were the chances the hunter would let that happen?

Fuck all. But sitting around doing nothing wasn't helping either.

Grinding his teeth against the pain, he straightened to his feet and shuffled over to the bars. "Hey!"

His shout bounced around the emptiness.

"Hey, fuckwit?" he yelled, pressing his palm to his side. It didn't help the pain, in fact, it made it worse. But it did feed his anger.

Anger was good. Nim always told him he was too damn slow to anger. He'd told her, more than once, an angry dire wolf was no one's idea of a safe time. His fellow Guarded Souls team mates didn't need a dire wolf with a hairline trigger of a temper in the communal staff kitchen when someone left dirty dishes in the sink, or decided his lunch looked more inviting than theirs—something that happened more than once. A dire wolf could decimate a vampire in a split second, devour a wiccan in even less time, and rip apart a dream walker without raising a sweat. Sure, a pissed-off dire wolf may not stand up so well against an angel and a djinn, but Nathanial and James weren't always around to keep the others safe. Better to stay calm than to anger.

When he'd pointed that out to Nim, the wiccan had cocked an eyebrow. "Kitt, all that pent up anger you've been suppressing is going to make you explode one day. I hope to hell I'm there to see it. It'll be a thing of beauty."

A thing of beauty.

If he could get the hunter in the cage with him now... yeah, *that* would be a thing of beauty.

He pressed his hand harder to his side, sinking into the hot ropes of agony lashing at him.

Feed your anger. Let it free. Use it.

He'd kept his anger under almost as tight a leash as he did his wolf. Had done for centuries now. His unchecked anger was scary.

"Hey!" he bellowed again, wrapping a hand around a bar. Icy pain sliced into his palm and up his arm, clashing with the burning pain in his side.

Hissing out a laugh, he shook his head and rolled his shoulders. "Get your ass back in here, you chicken."

His shout faded away to nothing.

No door opened anywhere in the blackness. No footsteps sounded in the room.

Fuck. How did he get out of here if he couldn't see any—

"Oh, you idiot," he mumbled. Releasing the bar, he clapped his hands together in a sharp report. Twice.

Bright white light flooded the vacuous space.

Cringing against the sudden onslaught, he scanned the area.

Definitely empty. The hunter had placed the cage in what appeared to be the center of an abandoned warehouse, or at least one long neglected. Or maybe a gutted factory. The high windows were mostly broken, boarded up or masked in black tape, and the only door seemed to be one large metal roller door in the middle of what felt like the north wall.

Kitt studied it. In the bottom left corner was a normal, hinged door, also closed. The only easy point of entry. And exit.

If he could just get out of the fucking cage...

"Hey," he yelled.

Pain washed over him, his head swam and he coughed. Blood splattered the floor.

Shit.

What did he do? He didn't have the time for someone at Guarded Souls to miss him, and he had no way of getting out of the cage.

Get the hunter back in here. Somehow force him or provoke him to open the cage. It's your only option.

"Hey," he roared.

The room spun. Black swirls of pain filled his vision. His knees crumpled and he hit the floor. Hard.

"Hey," he called again, although it came out a wobbly, watery rasp.

The door didn't open.

His vision blurred, black swirls tangling with black swirls...

Fuck.

After all these centuries, this is how he died? In a cage while a hunter ate dinner.

"I'm not afraid of dying," he mumbled. "I just don't want to be there when it happens."

Who had said that? Some British comedian Kade had introduced him to decades ago? The problem with living a long time, you forgot a lot of—

Something dark moved high in the corner of the room.

Wriggled through one of the broken windows.

"What the..." Kitt mumbled, frowning at the shape as it clung to the bottom of the window and then, with a muttered *shit*, dropped to the floor.

No, not a shape. A person. Dressed in dark-green camouflage gear.

A short person.

Five foot four. Maybe shorter. It was hard to tell; not with the waves of pain blurring his vision.

Squinting at the person now crouched on the floor against the far wall, he slowly shoved himself to his feet.

Was this the other person the hunter couldn't wait to show Kitt to? Was he about to be...poached by another *Monstrum Venator*?

Could this be his chance to get away?

How hard would it be to take out a hunter so—

"That was delicious."

The hunter's voice—filled with barbed glee—shattered the silence.

Spinning back to the door, Kitt locked his blurred stare on the tall, reedy man striding toward the cage.

"There's nothing quite like an In and Out burger to sate the appetite, don't you think?" The hunter stopped a foot away from the bars, smiled at Kitt, and held up a small bag. "Want some fries?"

Head swimming, Kitt bared his teeth. "Bite me."

The hunter shook the bag. "Not hungry?"

"I'm watching my weight," Kitt answered, although the words came out almost a slur. Blood coated his tongue. His breath gurgled. Whoever the new arrival was, they were running out of time to either kill him themselves, or...do whatever they were planning to do.

The hunter laughed. "You are so much fun, wolf. Seriously, I'm inclined to keep you all to myself. The bragging rights aren't worth missing out on this kind of *tet a tet*."

The camo-dressed, five-foot-four-maybe person slinked across the warehouse floor, coming up behind the hunter. Silent.

Kitt shot them a quick glance.

Short. Petite even.

Female?

Yes, female.

Female and...and...

Kitt's breath caught. What the fuck? He had to be seeing things. There was no way the woman creeping toward the hunter could be—

A soft crunch cracked the air and the woman froze, dropping her head. Stared at her foot.

The hunter stiffened. Began to turn around.

"How 'bout I shove those fries down your throat?" Kitt burst out, drilling his attention on the old bastard. Willing him to not look behind him. "Or up your ass. Chicken."

Scowl creasing his face more, the hunter took a step closer to the cage and jabbed an index finger at him. "I must admit, I'm getting tired of you calling me a chicken. Maybe you need a reminder of who's in charge here, wolf. And another dose of—"

A solid, meaty thud filled the room, and—eyes rolling back into his head—the hunter collapsed to the ground.

"Hi Kitt," the woman who'd climbed through the window whispered, her voice as shaky as her hands. "Umm...I bet you're wondering what I'm doing here?"

Amber Calegari, veterinarian, and—as of last week— the only human he'd considered asking out, stood staring at him, a rusty wrench in her white-knuckle grip, her chocolate-brown eyes wider than he'd ever seen them.

KEY. Where the hell is the key?

"Amber."

Digging around in the unconscious old guy pockets, Amber winced. Clearly Kitt hadn't been satisfied with her answer.

And really, did she blame him? Anyone with half a

brain would recognized "I was just driving by and saw you being dragged into this building" as complete bullshit.

Although, to be fair, *half* of her zero-planned explanation for why she happened to be here *was* actually accurate. She *had* watched the old dude dragging an unconscious Kitt into the building. She just hadn't been driving *by*. She'd actually been, well, *pursuing* the old dude.

Chasing after him after she'd seen him dragging Kitt into his car up in the Topanga Canyon hills.

Trying to explain why *she* was up in the hills, where Kitt had been in wolf form—wolf form! She'd finally witnessed him in wolf form!—was a tad problematic.

"Ah-ha!" She closed her fingers around the set of keys in Old Dude's inside jacket pocket and yanked them free.

A whiff of something not quite right followed them, like moth balls and an ulcerated wound and vanilla essence all mixed up together.

Scrunching up her nose, she jolted to her feet and waved the keys around in triumph, staring at them like they were the only thing in the room. "Found them."

At least the keys wouldn't stare back at her with contemplative suspicion.

She and Kitt had to move quickly. Who knew how long before the old guy regain consciousness. She'd never knocked someone out before. She'd once hit Mick hard enough to make him *almost* pass out, but that had been an accident. He'd been teaching her how to box and her wild haymaker had taken them both by surprise.

"Amber," Kitt murmured again.

She'd avoided looking at him since her blurted, poor excuse of an explanation. The doubt in his eyes had stabbed at her guilt, and any hope of saying anything else got knotted up with fear.

Lying to a paranormal creature wasn't smart. Especially not a paranormal creature who thought—thanks to everything she'd told him over the last six weeks—she was a veterinarian with no clue about what he truly was.

It also hadn't helped he was completely naked.

As soon as she opened the cage she'd give him the clothes she'd stuffed into the small pack on her back that morning.

Five hours ago she'd had no idea what exactly happened with his clothing when he shifted form. Hours of watching *True Blood* on HBO informed her shifters stripped before transforming, and her geek brain accepted that as the likely scenario even as her scientist brain kept flailing about the whole 'dire wolf shifter' scenario. Sitting in her motel room that morning, she'd extrapolated from her *True Blood* education that if she *did* bust Kitt Newton during his transformation from wolf to human like she planned, he'd be naked.

And as much as the human Kitt Newton pushed very feminine, very interested buttons in her—and whoa baby, *did* human Kitt push those buttons—she assumed he would *not* be pleased with their inevitable confrontation taking place while he wore no clothes. Hence her packing sweatpants and a T-shirt for him.

Sweatpants and a T-shirt she'd give him as soon as he stepped out of the cage.

The quick glimpse she'd allowed herself *before* refusing to look at him again though? Wow. Seriously, wow.

"I'm just going to..." She fumbled with the set of keys, flicking through the collection attached to the chain. Which one opened the cage?

At her feet, the old guy let out a fart.

Her heart skipped its way up her throat and she shot him a harried glance. Still unconscious. Good.

"Maybe this one," she muttered, selecting a particularly shiny key. The cage looked new, the bars pristine and the lock without any signs of frequent use. If *she* were planning to catch a dire wolf shifter, she'd have to get a cage made so it stood to reason Old Dude had as well.

Although something about him made her skin crawl, and it wasn't just the fact he'd somehow managed to catch and cage Kitt.

"Amber..."

Pain threaded through Kitt's groan, enough to unfurl a cold ribbon of fear and worry in her stomach. She looked up from the lock and found his gaze trained on her.

Oh God, confirmation he *was* a paranormal creature hadn't changed the fact he was the sexiest thing she'd ever seen.

"Hurry," he rasped, lowering his gaze. She followed where he was now looking, and gasped at the raw, angry wound on his side.

Throat thick, blood roaring in her ears, she returned her attention to the lock. Goddamn it, her hands were shaking so much she couldn't line up the freaking key.

Calm down. Just calm down. What would Mick say if he saw you so flustered?

Mick would freaking arrest her for break-and-enter, physical assault, and then throw her in a loony bin for insisting the man she was saving was a dire wolf shifter. Of the three of the Calegari siblings, the eldest was the most pragmatic. It came with being a forensic detective.

"When...we get out of here," Kitt's scratchy voice

sounded like a scream in the silence, "you're going to...to tell me exactly who you are."

Breath choking her, skin prickling, she met his gaze again.

The tiniest of smile played with his blood-flecked lips. "Because I don't...think you're..." His face scrunched up and he winced, buckling over as he pressed his hand to his side.

"Kitt?" she whispered, her stare locking on the fresh blood oozing from between his fingers.

He shook his head and, lurching sideways, looked at her again. "I don't think you're just the hot girl I met at the coffee house, are—"

He collapsed to the floor, a lump of muscle and sweat-slicked skin.

"Oh God, oh God." Heart hammering in her ears, Amber fumbled with the lock. "Oh God, Kitt? Kitt, wake up."

He didn't move.

Didn't even groan.

"Kitt?" Tears stung her eyes. She stabbed the key at the lock. Missed. Stabbed again. And again. "Kitt?"

Nothing.

"No no no no no."

Calm. Down!

Mick's low order reverberated through her head.

"Easy for you to say, big bro," she muttered, pulling a deep breath. And another.

On the third breath, hands steady, eyes burning, she slid the key into the lock and turned it.

"Yes!" she burst out, and then flung the old guy on the floor a look.

Still out cold.

Good.

Yanking open the cage door, she scrambled inside and clunked to her knees beside Kitt, grabbing at his shoulder. "Hey." She shook him. It was like shaking a mountain. "Wake up, Kitt. I'm not strong enough to drag you out of—"

"I'm...okay," he groaned, slowly planting his palms on the floor. "Help...me—"

"Up. Got it." She leapt to her feet, hooked her arms under his armpits and hauled him upward. She refused to acknowledge his naked body kept bumping and sliding against her. "Oh my God, you're heavy."

"Hey," he protested, the word part groan part chuckle, as he lurched sideways once again.

She grunted, pulled off balance by his momentum, and barely stopped him tumbling back to floor. Sweat trickled into her eyes. "This is *not* how I saw this rescue going."

With another part groan/part laugh, he rose to his feet again. But only just. "Aren't you a little short for a storm trooper?" he mumbled.

"If you can drop *Star Wars* quotes," she muttered, shooting Old Dude a worried glance, " you can walk out of here your—shit!" She grabbed at Kitt as he began to crumple. "Alright, big guy. Work with me, okay?"

Snagging one thick, muscular arm, she draped it around her shoulders again. His weight threatened the strength of her own knees, but she ground her teeth. When she saw Ray next, she'd have to thank him for all the times he'd insisted she owed him a piggy-back after every piggy-back he'd given her. Of course, he'd stopped doing that when she was eleven, but still—muscle memory and all.

"Amber..." Kitt slurred as she began to move them both

toward the cage door. God, how was she going to get him to her rental? The Prius was on the other side of the warehouse's fence. Was there a wheelbarrow anywhere nearby? "Am…"

Am. He'd only started calling her Am two weeks ago during one of their "accidental" meetings. Back then, it had sent little licks of excitement and delight through her. A nickname. He'd given her nickname. After three weeks of "bumping into each other" and a week of sitting together and chatting after said "bumping" he'd given her a nickname. Now however…well, guilt was a sonofabitch emotion. Would he call her Am after he discovered what she'd really done?

You won't find out if you don't get him out of here alive. He has excessive bleeding, most likely internal injuries. He needs medical attention. ASAP.

Ray's voice that time. Ever the veterinarian.

"C'mon," she muttered, hitching Kitt's arm farther around her shoulders, and staggering toward the open cage door. "Let's go."

"Am…" he mumbled, the name barely more than a breath. "I was…going…to ask…you…"

Silence. Followed by his weight turning impossibly heavy.

"Hey?" She squeezed his wrist and shook him as well as she could, given she was damn near wearing him like a freaking cape. "Ask me what?"

He let out a weak grunt, eyes closed, head lulling. "Out."

Oh great. He had intended to ask her out. That's what she got for being so damn adorable anytime she "accidentally" ran into the coffee shop at the same time he did.

"C'mon guilt," she ground out, forcing her legs to keep moving, "give me strength."

Unless he means out as in let's get the hell out *of here?*

She dragged/carried him out of the cage. It took forever. On the floor, the old guy remained motionless. Shit, what if she'd killed him?

"*This* is why paleontologists don't deal with living people," she muttered. "Damn you, Sam Neill. I'll never trust you in a role again."

"I liked him in *The Hunt for the Wilderpeople*," Kitt mumbled, his weight lightening a little around her shoulders.

Twisting her head, she frowned at him.

Pain etched his face. His eyes were squeezed shut. But he didn't bare down on her as much as he had before. Good. That was good.

Of course, they weren't even halfway across the warehouse floor but still...

Baby steps. Baby steps.

"How are you feeling?" she asked, returning her stare to the massive roller door. If she could just get him out, she could lock the door somehow. Trap the old guy inside. Then she could leave Kitt somewhere safe and go get the Prius.

"Not...good." He hissed as her right knee buckled, sending her shoulder jolting up into his armpit. "Ouch."

"Sorry. You're heavier than you look, and you look like you'd give a grizzle a run for its money."

Another one of those chuckling groans fell from him. "You have...no..."

His head lulled forward and he turned to a deadweight, rolling forward and crumpling her to the ground with him.

"No no no," she yelped. Pain detonated in her knees, up her back. "Shit, I can't—"

"Hey!" a furious voice shouted behind them. "What the fuck do you think you're doing?"

Shit.

Shoving against Kitt's motionless weight, Amber scrambled to her feet. Fell over. Scrambled upright again. Grabbed at his wrist and tried to drag him, throwing a wild grin at the elderly man shuffling toward them.

Old Dude. Back in the land of the living. Again.

Shit.

The old guy shuffled faster, rubbing at the back of his head, glare fixed on her. "Stop right there. Who are you?"

"Hey," she called back, pulse pounding as she pulled harder on Kitt's wrist. Nope. He wasn't budging. Shit. At least the old man looked easy to beat in a fight. He was still wobbly on his feet, and seriously, how old *was* he? Seventy? "I'm glad you're awake. I just found you both unconscious here and figured I better get you both help." Talk about awesome thinking on her feet. Maybe she *was* action-movie-heroine worthy after all? "Are you okay? What's with the—"

Old Dude lowered his arm from behind his head to reveal a curved dagger as long as her forearm in his grip.

"Whoa whoa whoa." She dropped Kitt's wrist and waved her hands in front of her. "What are you *doing*? I'm just trying to help."

Clearly Old Dude didn't believe her. With a snarl, he shambled quicker toward her, swinging the dagger around in his grip like he knew how to use it. Which he probably did. Just because he was old didn't mean he was feeble. He had dragged Kitt into his car, after all. She'd seen him do that, and she now had first-hand experience at how freaking difficult that was to do.

Damn it, why hadn't she stuck the wrench she'd found, the one she'd knocked him out with, in her back pocket? What was the point of having camo gear if she didn't make use of the pouches?

Stepping over Kitt's inert body, she nudged him with her heel, and threw a smile at the old guy. "Hi, I'm Amber," she blurted. *Tell your attacker your name. Make them see you as a person.* Mick told her that constantly, every time he insisted on teaching her more self-defense. "What's your name?"

Of course, she could outrun the old git. But she wasn't leaving Kitt.

"Manson," Old Dude provided, flashing her a smile. Shit, he shuffled fast for a recently knocked-out geriatric.

"As in Marilyn?"

His smile grew sharkish. He flicked the knife around in his grip with an evil flourish. Guess arthritis wasn't a problem for him. "More like Charles," he said.

Closer now. So close.

Too close. The unsettling scent of vanilla, moth balls and bile trickled into her breath. Crouching lower, shielding Kitt as much as she could, she waved her hands in front of her again. "Can we just talk about this? Before you try to kill me?"

He chortled, coming to a halt. "I'm not going to kill you, girly."

She blinked. "You're not?"

"I'm going to keep you as food." He threw a look at Kitt on the floor behind her. "For him."

"Wh-what?" Oh crap. Crap. She nudged Kitt with her heel again. Willed him to regain consciousness.

What's he going to do? He's barely alive. You got yourself into this situation. Get yourself out of it.

"Do you know what kind of creature you've got there, girly?" Manson pointed the tip of the dagger at Kitt. "What kind of monster you're trying to save?"

"Dire wolf shifter."

The words left her on a steady statement, and they did exactly what she wanted them to do: shock old Mr. Manson.

He blanched. "Dire wolf shifter. How do you know that?"

"Well, *Canis Dirus* if you want to use the correct scientific term," she went on, affecting her most Professor Calegari tone. How she could talk with her heart hammering away in her throat the way it was, was beyond her comprehension. "Although technically it'd be *canis dirus shifter*, given he's a...well, a dire wolf shifter. I don't think there's a Latin word for shifter. It's been a while since I had to expand my Latin vocabulary. I'll look it up when I get home. Unless you'll let me get my phone? I've got a translation app on it. Is the cell service here okay?"

Manson gaped at her. And then scowled. "Are you a fellow guild member?"

Guild?

"Yeah." She nodded with a cheery smile. "Yeah yeah. Definitely."

What was she *doing*?

He narrowed his eyes. "Prove it."

Shit.

"Umm..." She licked her lips, mouth dry and extended her right hand toward him. "Super-secret handshake time?"

Oh God. If Ray or Mick or Sam Neill could see her now.

Manson's eyebrows shot up? "Super-secret... You're not a member of the guild, are you."

Dropping her hand, she grimaced. "No."

He smiled again. "In that case, I'm going to enjoy seeing you—"

Something shoved Amber aside. Something large and solid and hard and growling and naked.

Kitt.

He threw himself at Manson. Slammed into the older man. Smashed him to the floor.

Manson gibbered and bucked and squealed and thrashed about beneath his pinning weight, but Kitt didn't flinch. Didn't pause. He grabbed the old guy's wrist and, with one fluid thrust, sank the dagger into Manson's throat.

Amber screamed. Slapped her hands to her mouth. Screamed into her palms.

Blood spurt from the side of Manson's neck, drenching the blade's hilt and Kitt's hand. The old guy flailed about for a few seconds more, stare locked on Kitt, hands clawing at his bare shoulders, and then, as if all the bones had suddenly left his body, he went limp.

And silent.

Eyes burning, breath trapped in her throat, Amber froze. Watched Kitt's bare back and shoulders rise and fall with breath after ragged breath.

"K...Kitt?" she whispered.

He snapped his head toward her, eyes glowing with unnatural golden light, and what little breath she had in her lungs burst from her in a gasp.

"I gotta..." she muttered, and then sprinted for the door.

Oh God. Oh God, what...what...

"Am?"

Her feet tangled at his groan. She stumbled to a halt and, heart racing, looked back over her shoulder.

"Am," he said again, eyes no longer glowing. "I'm..."

The dagger slipped from his grip, clattering to the floor beside Manson's still body, and he collapsed to the floor.

Amber flinched and, with a roll of her eyes and a ragged sigh, hurried back to him. "Crap." She crouched beside him and slung his limp arm around her shoulders. "Bet Alan Grant never has to put up with this."

Bracing herself, she dragged him up off the floor, and fixed her stare on the roller door.

"*Or* Sam Neill. I better get a whole freaking edition of *Scientific American* dedicated to my paper on you," she muttered. "Or if nothing else, a freaking gazillion Instagram likes."

2

_____

Moving.

Was he moving? The sensation in his gut told him he was.

In a car? Maybe.

But he was lying down. Or was he?

Opening his eyes, he winced at the bright sunlight stabbing at him, and shifted on the seat.

Seat. Car seat. The back seat.

Someone had laid him out on the back seat of a car.

Whose car? It smelled new, and at the same time undercut with multiple scents of sweat and body odor. Like a rental.

How had he got here?

Monstrum Venator...cage...drugged...

Amber...

Amber had freed him. How the hell had the woman he'd met at his favorite café rescued him from the _Monstrum Venator_? How had they got away? Had she—

An image of the old man filled his head; splayed out on

the ground of the warehouse, the hilt of a knife protruding from the side of his wrinkly neck.

An icy chill rippled over Kitt and his gut churned. He'd...he'd killed the hunter.

He'd come to just enough to hear the *Monstrum Venator* threaten Amber and he'd snapped and—

Killed him. Lost your temper and killed him.

He sat up. Or tried to. Pain wracked his body. A fire burned in his side. He groaned, slumping back down to the seat.

"We're almost there," Amber's worried voice floated from the front of the car. "Try not to move."

Wincing again, he squinted up at the back of the seat in front of him. "Almost where?" The words scratched at his dry throat. "How long have I been out?"

Silence.

"Am?"

She shifted in the driver's seat. "A little while."

Gritting his teeth again, he moved his hand to his side, and paused when his brain—dulled by pain, the hunter's drugs, the dragon's bone, or maybe the whole fucking lot —noticed a blanket covered him, the kind found in emergency First-aid kits.

Camo gear, first-aid kits, knocking out Monstrum Venators... *You need answers.*

Pressing his palm to the wound in his side—Hell, how many Band-aids had she stuck over it?—he inched his way into an upright position. Waves of giddiness crashed over him. His stomach lurched. Pain lashed at him. Gripping the edge of the blanket with a shaky hand, he found her reflection in the car's rearview mirror.

Their gazes connected for a heartbeat. Worry swam in

her brown eyes; eyes he'd drawn to mind more than once these last few weeks.

"You shouldn't be sitting up," she admonished, a frown tugging at her forehead.

Her faint Italian accent tickled something deep in him. He may be dying, but the soft inflection he'd noticed the first time they spoke over a month and a half ago still had the ability to stoke a base male response in him. Every time they'd bumped into each other in the café, he'd hung on her every word, the sound of her voice, the soft lilt in her words, the mischief in her eyes... all stirring a reaction in him. One he'd tried to ignore for weeks. Until he accepted the fact he couldn't ignore it any more.

And then the shit hit the fan for James and he'd rushed to his friend's aid.

And *then* he'd got shot by the *Monstrum Venator*.

Pulling a slow breath, he studied what he could see of her face in the small mirror. "Tell me who you really are, Amber."

Her eyes flicked to his for a second. "I'm...just Amber."

He snorted, winced as angry pain sheared through him again, and shook his head. "No you're not. Where are we going?"

She kept her stare on the road, changing lanes with jerky haste. "Somewhere to fix you up."

"A hospital?"

Her eyebrows dipped. "No."

With a wobbly chuckle, he leant toward the driver's seat, even as his body screamed in protest. "Your clinic?"

Her eyes flicked to his again for a split second. "My what?"

A knot twisted in his gut. "I thought so." He slumped

back into the seat, closing his eyes. "You're not a veterinarian, are you."

"Crap," she muttered.

Letting out a snort, he shook his head against the seat. "Of course, the first woman I'm remotely interested in turns out to be a..." He opened his eyes and studied her reflection. "What are you? A *Monstrum Venator* as well?"

"A what?"

He closed his eyes again. He'd never heard anyone sound more clueless, and he'd lived for over four hundred years.

"Okay, so not a *Monstrum Venator.*" He shifted on the seat, wincing as a bolt of pain sank deep into his side.

"What's a *Monstrum Venator*? It's sounds Latin."

"A hunter." The word left him on a flat murmur. It hurt to breathe. To sit. To remain motionless. To fight against the car's jerky, uneven momentum. Whatever she was, she wasn't a smooth driver. At least, she wasn't right at this moment.

He found her reflection in the mirror again.

"Are they the guild the old dude was talking about?" she asked, focus trained on the road.

How much did she know? And how much did he reveal? "They are. They hunt for the sport of the kill, and for some, bragging rights."

Another frown pulled at her forehead. "So he caught you to kill you? Or to brag about catching you?"

How did he answer this? "I don't know."

"Possibly because he knows what you are," she said, flicking him a look.

His chest tightened. "And what *am* I?"

She returned her attention to the road. "We're here."

She maneuvered the car into a sharp right, the

momentum jolting him sideways in the backseat. A wave of black pain crashed over him and he bit back a growl, clawing at the blanket sliding off him instead.

A slight bump juddered through the car—the curb? A driveway?—and he winced, fresh pain making his head swim. Damn it, he'd run out of time. He still knew nothing about her, or where she'd brought him.

Wherever it was, he'd subdue her somehow, find a phone and call—

The car door opened beside him and she stuck her head in a little. "Don't freak out when you see the sign, okay?"

"What sign?" He frowned, trying to see past her as she leant further in. "Where—"

"I promise I'll try not to hurt you," she said, awkwardly sliding her arm around his back. "But you're going to have to help me get you inside."

He pulled away, snatched at the blanket as it tried to slide off him again, and winced as his body erupted in pain. Not just his side; his body.

Black swirls filled his vision. The world spun.

A low groan tore through the car and it took his brain a second to realize it was him.

"Kitt," Amber whispered, leaning closer to him, her arm completely around his back. "Trust me. Please?"

He lifted his gaze to her. Locked his stare on hers. And nodded. "O…"

The rest of the word faded. Everything faded. Swam into a blur. And then nothing.

"I can't tell you."

Amber's voice—agitated and worried—trickled through the nothing.

"You're kidding?" a male voice—deep, just as agitated, but also a little humored—followed. "You can't tell me? Why?"

Kitt forced his eyes open. And flinched as sharp white light assaulted them.

Operating table lights. Four of them.

The unmistakable smell of disinfectant slid into his nose, tainted by the distinct odor of feces. Not human though. Animal.

He twisted on the cold metal slab beneath him, biting back a hiss of pain. Something tugged at his waist and a distant part of his brain told him he was dressed in sweat-pants. Where the hell was—

"Oh thank God," a sharp breath burst from Amber. "He's awake."

"Good," the male voice grumbled. "Now I might get some answers."

Still squinting against the glaring light, Kitt turned to the owner of the grumble.

A man stood beside the slab, frowning down at him.

"Be nice, Ray," Amber ordered.

Ray—whoever Ray was—snorted. Tall and solid, with a hooked nose, blue eyes, and shaggy dark blond hair, he looked...familiar. Somehow. "You rock up to my clinic with a naked, strange guy whose clearly been shot, almost three hours after you hung up on me, refusing to tell me why? A guy who looks like he could bench press a semi-trailer and growls like an animal whenever I touch him?" He flicked her a look, and a tight finger of jealousy traced up Kitt's spine at the love suddenly filling his face. "Yeah, *nice* is not the emotion I'm thinking of channeling right now."

Amber narrowed her eyes and jabbed a finger at him across Kitt's chest. "Don't go all Mick on me, Raymond."

"Raymond? Full name time?" Ray snorted again. "Just how much shit have you got yourself into?"

"Hello?" Kitt rasped, looking up at them. Who'd put the sweatpants on him? Where had they come from? "Confused, shot guy on the table."

Two sets of concerned eyes swung to him, and he got it. Why Ray looked oddly familiar.

Related. Whoever Ray was, he was related to Amber.

"How do you feel?" Amber asked, fingers skimming over his side.

"Watch the bandaging, sis," Ray admonished.

Sis.

Brother, then. *Big* brother, going by the crow's feet at the corners of his eyes and undeniable protective tone.

Ignoring them both, Kitt pushed himself up onto his elbows. And stopped as a world of agony detonated in his side, up his arm, and down into his gut and groin.

"Take it easy." Ray pressed a gentle but firm palm to Kitt's bare chest. "I removed a bullet casing in your side, but I have no clue what else is in there or what you were even shot with. There's some serious shit still in there I've never seen before."

"Dragon's bone," Kitt mumbled, head swimming as he slumped back down to the slab.

"Dragon's bone?" Ray repeated, eyebrows shooting up. "What the hell's dragon bone? Some type of buckshot?"

Amber let out a groan, scrunched up her face, and shook her head. "Ray, just... Is there anything else you can give him?"

Ray crossed his arms and glared at her. "An interrogation?"

"Ha ha. Funny." Amber rolled her eyes and crossed her own arms. If Kitt wasn't in so much pain, he'd laugh. Feisty Amber was a revelation.

"I want answers, sis," Ray grumbled.

Ditto, Kitt thought.

"Otherwise lover-boy here can suffer."

"Hey," Amber spluttered. "Who says—"

"I'm not her—" Kitt said.

"Yeah yeah," Ray raised both hands. "Whatever." He fixed Kitt in a steady stare. "But here's the thing. A few hours ago, my little sister right here abruptly ended a call with me, for which the subject of conversation was *why* she requested a DNA search from her other big brother, and then she shows up here with you in toe, unconscious and bleeding and almost on death's door, desperate for me to save your life." His eyes narrowed. "And up until her arrival, I had money on Amber being married solely to her work."

Kitt's chest tightened as his stare slowly slid to Amber.

She jerked her gaze away, frowning. Fidgeting.

"DNA search?" he asked, trying to sit up again. "*Whose*—"

His side erupted in agony. Damn it, how soon before he started healing?

"DNA?" Ray retrieved something from the counter behind him. "My question exactly."

He turned back to the operating table, syringe in hand.

"Whoa whoa whoa." Kitt threw himself off the table. Pain engulfed him, like molten blades slicing into raw flesh, like muscles torn apart. He thudded to the floor, smacking into Amber and knocking her backward.

"Hey!" Ray shouted, vaulting the table.

He landed on the floor directly in front of Kitt, grabbed

Amber's arm and swung to glare at Kitt. "What the fuck, dude?"

Rising to his feet—wobbly and breathless and body screaming—Kitt stared at him. "Before anyone sticks a needle into me, I need answers."

Ray frowned. "Needle phobia? Really? A big guy like you?"

Muscles coiling, Kitt hunched his shoulders, fighting the urge to pass out. Deep inside, his wolf stirred...and fell silent and quiet again. He ground his teeth. The next time he saw the *Monstrum Venator* he was going to—

You killed him already, remember?

His breath caught in his throat. Shit. He had.

There'd been nothing, not even pain, and then the old bastard's voice cut through the nothingness, threatening Amber, and he'd...what? Not wolfed out, but something else.

He'd killed the hunter, sunk the man's own dagger into his throat and...

Woke up in the back seat of Amber's car.

His knees crumpled and he grabbed the edge of the metal table, eyes closed, head spinning.

"Kitt." Amber grabbed at his shoulder. Steadying him. Halting his fall. "I've got you."

Waves of nausea rolled through him. The inferno in his side bloomed hotter.

...hollow-tip silver bullet... the *Monstrum Venator's* boast snaked through his head. *...filled with ground dragon bone, plus a little secret ingredient, and coated in the very compound preventing you from shifting...*

The dragon bone had attacked his *croi*, crippling its magic, and the compound retarded his ability to shift form. But what was the *little secret ingredient*? What had it done to him?

And now you'll never find out because you killed the bastard. Let your temper rule you and now you're screwed.

"His name's Kitt?" Ray's voice rumbled through the ocean of pain engulfing him. "Really? After the car?"

"You are so old, brother," Amber muttered, inching Kitt back up to his feet.

He swung her a blurry look, and then heaved himself back up onto the table, wincing as he went. She'd saved him from the hunter. He had to trust she hadn't done so just to kill him, or have her brother do so.

But why did *she save you? She hasn't told you that yet.*

"It's going to be okay," she murmured, hands fluttering over his body as he stretched out onto his back. "Ray's the best in town."

"Best what?" he mumbled, closing his eyes as fresh pain lashed through him.

"Veterinarian," Ray answered. "No, I don't know why Amber has brought you to me instead of a doctor either, but she assures me I'm what you need right now."

Veterinarian.

Opening his eyes, he frowned up at her.

She met his gaze for a second before sliding hers away. "I didn't know if you were going to..."

She stopped, flicked him a quick look and chewed on her bottom lip.

Going to what? Shift form? Did she know?

Did she know what he was?

"Poop yourself," she mumbled, cheeks growing pink. "Veterinarians are better at dealing with poop than doctors."

"What the hell are you talking about, sis?"

Kitt dragged his stare from her, and fixed it on Ray. "What are you going to do with that needle?"

The question came out a raspy breath. Each word sank through him like a knife.

"Tranc you." Ray grinned.

Kitt shot up his eyebrows. Shit, that hurt as well.

"Ray," Amber growled.

"Kidding." Ray chuckled. "I'm going to try to numb your side more, alleviate the pain so you can move."

Move was good. He needed to deal with the *Monstrum Venator*'s body. He needed to get hold of someone from Guarded Souls. He needed to find out if James was alive. He had to assume he was: djinn were damn near almost impossible to kill.

He needed answers from Amber, and clearly she wasn't ready to give them in front of her brother.

Who was a veterinarian.

She'd brought him to a veterinarian.

He didn't know whether to laugh, or be insulted.

A sharp click drew his attention back to Ray.

"This is probably going to hurt," Ray said, squirting a little of the clear fluid in the syringe out. "But after—"

Music started playing from Amber's hip pocket, loud and jarring and too catchy for his current mental and physical condition.

"Is that Mick? You still got 'Bad Boys' as his ring tone?" Ray asked, as Amber yanked her phone free. "He will kill you."

"Mick can bite me," she shot back, swiping her thumb over the screen.

Kitt lay motionless, watching her. Who was Mick?

"Heya, big bro," Amber said, cheesy smile plastered on her face and in her voice. "What's—"

She stopped. Frowned.

Flicked a glance at him, then Ray, then the floor. "What do you mean, *tracked* me? I'm not five, you—"

An invisible band wrapped Kitt's chest. Forcing himself into an upright position, he slid Ray his own quick look. Guilt swam on the man's face.

But why?

"No, I *don't* understand," Amber said. "I can come to LA if I want to. Why would you keep track of where I— Where are you? You're where? Are you *really* calling to give me a lecture from a *crime* scene?"

Kitt's gut clenched. What was her other brother saying?

"Why are..." She threw up her free hand. "Oh my God, I don't want to know that... How *much* blood? Wait, *where* are you again?"

She looked at Kitt again, and his breath caught in his throat at the fear in her eyes.

"You need to get back to work, Mick," she muttered. "And stop treating me like a little kid."

Shoving the phone back in her pocket, she dropped her stare to the floor for a second before letting out a choppy breath and looking at Kitt. "Um, that old guy who had you in the cage? From the guild?"

"The *Monstrum Venator*?"

"The what?" Ray said. "The who? The *where*?"

Amber ignored him. "Yeah, him. As it turns out, Mick —my other brother—was called into the crime scene at the warehouse. That's where he just called me from, lecturing me about... Actually, that doesn't matter. Mick is an over-protective pain in the ass."

"Hey!" Ray burst out.

Amber rolled her eyes. "It's true. So are you. Anyways,"

she turned her attention back to Kitt, "it seems the old guy's body has gone. Missing. From the warehouse. And the bloody footprints on the floor indicate he walked out."

Fuck.

"We've gotta go." He threw himself off the operating table, snagged her arm, and hurried toward the only door he could see. "Now."

"What the hell?" Ray gaped at him, at Amber, and back to him. "What do you mean, go?"

"Are we—" Amber began, taking Kitt's arm and gently slinging it around her shoulder. Without arguing, without question. She trusted him. Already. Who the hell was she?

"Not safe," he finished. *In a shit load of danger* was more accurate, but he couldn't say that. Not in front of Ray. The veterinarian would probably tranquilize him in a foolish attempt to save his sister.

A sister now the target of a *MonstrumVvenator* who should be dead.

He needed to get Amber away from here now. For Ray's sake and hers.

If the hunter *was* alive—and Kitt's gut told him he was —the bastard would be tracking them.

Supporting his own weight as much as her could, he fixed Ray in a steady look. "I'll explain later, I promise, but you need to close the clinic now. Send your staff home and—"

"It's just me," Ray cut in. "It's Sunday. I'm only here because Amber called and told me she had an emergency. I thought she'd hit a stray dog with the rental."

A twisted part of Kitt almost laughed. If James were here, the djinn—who called him Rover most of the time— would be delighted.

"Good," he said, shifting his arm around Amber's

shoulder. A shard of pain sank into his side and he hissed. How the hell was he going to fight off the hunter if he couldn't heal? "Lock up, and go somewhere really public. Middle of a shopping mall, the corner of Hollywood and Vine, anywhere really busy. The more people, the better. And stay clear of any tall old, white guys who might approach you."

Ray blinked. It was better than being gaped out, but not much. "What?" He turned to Amber. "What the hell have you got yourself into, sis?"

Flicking Kitt a quick glance, she frowned at her brother. "We have to go, Ray. Please, just do what Kitt says. Or go see Mick. You'll be safe with him. Just…don't tell him what's going—"

"Stop." Ray shook his head, glaring at them both. "This is insanity. I'm not letting you go anywhere. Not with this guy. He's almost dead, for Chrissake."

Kitt ground his teeth. Inside, his wolf paced. Snarled.

"Ray, please." Amber tightened her grip on Kitt's hand. "You don't—"

"If you *are* in danger, he's not going to be able to protect you," Ray went on, face growing red. Anger and fear leeched from him. Kitt tasted it on the air.

His wolf snarled again, even as his head swam. Hell, when had the room become so hot? Every breath his pulled burned his lungs.

"Ray," Amber said again. "Please trust me. You need—"

"No." Ray pointed a finger at her. Kitt didn't miss the hypodermic needle still gripped in his hand. "I am calling Mick. I'm telling him—"

A growl tore from Kitt. Not even close to human in sound.

The fire burning through him ignited. A red haze filled his vision. Blurred it.

Everything moved. No, *he* moved. Fast. Sharp.

Pain detonated through him again, just as a jolt shuddered up his arm and into his shoulder, and Amber cried, "No!".

A solid thud filled the room, his shoulder screamed in agony, and the red haze evaporated.

Kitt blinked, his head swimming. What...why did he feel like...

He staggered sideways, catching himself on the operating table just as his foot stumbled against something.

"Ray?" Amber cried, dropping to her knees.

"Am," he mumbled, trying to track her move. Hell, he felt like he was being torn apart. "Am, we have to..."

His vision focused again, and his gut rolled.

Ray lay on the floor, eyes closed, blood trickling from a small gash beside his mouth. A bruise bloomed on his jaw, purple and angry, just near his chin.

"What..." His gut churned again, and he gripped the table tighter.

Had he done that?

"Ray?" Amber shook her brother's arm, and then glared up at Kitt. "Why did you do that?"

"I don't..." Squeezing his own eyes shut, he rubbed at his face. "There's something..." He dropped his hand and fixed her with a steady look. "I need a phone. Now. Before I pass out."

Eyes narrowing, she studied him for a split second before digging a smartphone from one of the pockets of her camo pants and thrusted it up at him.

"Is his jaw broken?" he asked, nodding at the motionless Ray as he took the phone.

In peak, uninjured health, he could punch through a concrete pillar. A human's jaw didn't stand a chance if he didn't hold back.

Glare returning, she touched Ray's jaw with tentative fingers. "No. I don't think so."

"Good." A tiny thread of relief unfurled through him. It wasn't much, but it was something. Turning his attention to the phone, he stabbed a number into her phone.

On the first ring, a deep, smooth voice said "Guarded Souls."

"Kade," Kitt said, closing his eyes again.

"Where the fuck are you?" the vampire asked with deadly calm.

He flicked Amber a quick look. "Address?"

She gave it to him, voice barely a whisper.

"Did you get that?" he asked back into the phone.

"I did," Kade replied. Now what's going on"

"I'll explain later." A wave of blackness swirled through his vision and he squeezed his eyes shut again. "Is James okay?"

"He is. Worried sick about you though."

Kitt snorted. "Knew the bastard would be. Get him or Nathanial here ASAP please. And I mean, ASAP. Or Christen or Dak if you can't get hold of them although they won't get here as fast, and protect the unconscious man lying on the floor until you hear from me."

"The unconscious man," Kade repeated. "Human or—"

"Human," Kitt said, opening his eyes and looking at Amber's motionless brother. "His name's Ray and he's going to be pissed when he comes to."

∾

THANK God he'd had the foresight to dose up on his curative elixir after eating his burger. If not...

A shudder rocked through Manson. Being killed by the very creature he hunted wasn't the ignoble way he wanted to go. The wound in his neck itched, even if blood no longer oozed from it.

Every time he found his fingers scraping over the crusting, congealing gash however, he drew an image of the monster responsible for it in his head. And the bitch who helped him.

Was she human? She hadn't behaved like a shifter of any kind back in the warehouse, or any other type of inhuman monster for that matter.

Lowering his hand from the side of his neck, he balled his fists. He'd never hunted a human before.

He pictured her in his mind, standing over the dire wolf, protecting it...

Hunting humans was against the guild's code of conduct. If he killed her when he tracked down the dire wolf, he'd be exorcised from the *Monstrum Venator*.

The female lifted her head in his mind and looked directly at him. *Then don't kill me*, she said silently.

"That could work," he murmured, meeting his own gaze in the grimy bathroom mirror once more.

Capture them both. Cage the monster again, and...cage the woman?

Yes, that would also work. Separately, of course. Keep them both alive until the fresh suppression serum he would injected into the wolf again on capture wore off. Cut into the human bitch until she was nothing more than walking-talking-crying chum, and then open both their cages.

Watch as the starving monster shifted into dire wolf

form and ran her down. Slit the dire wolf open as it gorged on her carcass.

Film the whole moment.

Sell the footage to those fellow guild members who appreciated such artistry.

Of course, before he did that, he'd have to let XI see the dire wolf. Prove he'd captured it.

The other guild member still gloated of his succubus kill to Manson whenever they interacted. The successful hunt and kill of a dire wolf shifter would shut him up.

Lowering his attention to his neck, he inspected the wound made by his own dagger.

Almost healed.

Good.

The curative elixir was doing its job nicely. It had taken him centuries to perfect its formula—a little bit of dark magic mixed with a little bit of archaic science and a lot of unicorn marrow—but it was worth it. It kept him young, after all. And alive.

If the guild found out, however...

Curling his lip, he turned from the mirror and strode from the motel room's small bathroom. The *Monstrum Venator* had a strict no-magic for personal use or gain policy. If his fellow members ever discovered his secret he'd become a target.

Hence changing his identity every fifty years or so, a procedure he'd have to complete again soon.

But not until after he successfully hunted the dire wolf. Adding that impressive kill would be the perfect swan-song for Guild Member K5's already imposing kill-count.

Then hurry up and find the creature. Before the suppression serum leaves the wolf's system completely. The chances of taking it by surprise again in either human or wolf form are non-existence. Especially if the human bitch is helping.

An image of the woman filled his head again.

Perhaps, instead of feeding her to the dire wolf, he could whip up a concoction and use it on her? Something to physically transform her into, say...a vampire—he had vials of vampire blood in cold storage he'd been wanting to experiment with. Transform her, let her loose up in the hills where he'd shot the dire wolf, and hunt her.

A thick chuckle bubbled up through his chest. That could be fun.

Not as profitable as selling footage of her being eaten by the dire wolf, to be sure, but a lot more fun.

Yes, that's what he would do.

Transform her, and hunt her. Another kill to add to his enviable list.

But first, he had to find them both, which should be relatively easy. The human bitch had been in a car; he'd seen the tire tracks in the dirt and despite the derelict appearance of the warehouse, he'd equipped it with a state-of-the-art security system the day he bought it; the day *after* he'd arrived in LA.

He hated the West Coast. Rarely came here. The inhuman creatures found in LA were cliched and unex-citing and not worth his time and skill. But discovering there was a living dire wolf shifter in LA was more than enough reason to come here. He'd set up camp, and prepared for the capture and the kill. Once the warehouse was ready, he'd begun to hunt the dire wolf in earnest.

He hadn't expected the creature to be rescued. Thank fuck for CCTV cameras. Their footage would reveal not only what kind of car the bitch had been driving but its plates.

"So let's begin." Lowering himself into the room's only seat—a frayed armchair that should have been sent to landfill a long time ago—he opened his laptop and began.

Find the car. Find the female. Find the—

His phone rang.

Putting aside his laptop, he plucked his phone up from the arm rest and arched an eyebrow. Why was Xɪ calling him?

Be careful.

They'd known of each other—as all guild members did—for many years now, however they'd only started to interact when Xɪ challenged his status as one of, if not *the* best on the *Monstrum Venator*'s forum. "Yes?"

"You've got something, haven't you."

It wasn't a question.

"Something significant." Envy threaded through Xɪ's deep voice. Was it naturally that deep, or did he use a voice modulator during their communication? It was possible. Likely, even.

Settling back into the grubby armchair, he chuckled. "Yes."

"This is why you're in LA?"

His heart slammed up into his throat. "Why do you assume I'm in LA? It's a God-awful city. And the hunt is substandard."

Xɪ's laugh rumbled through the connection. "I know exactly where you are, K."

He grew still. What game was Xɪ trying to play? Intimidation?

"In fact, I know what you ate for breakfast this morning. Fries? Really? I must admit, I pegged you for more of an Olive Garden type of diner than In-and-Out."

"What do you want, Xɪ?" he asked. Keep calm. He had

to keep calm. Couldn't give Xi the satisfaction of seeing him blink.

"I want to know where it is."

"Where *what* is?"

Xi laughed.

A chill rippled up Manson's back. The other guild member had always come across as a tad narcissistic—most *Monstrum Venator* were—but the smug menace in that laugh was on a different level.

"Whatever it is you're hunting here. I think you had it, but it got away. Where is it? *What* is it?"

"You think I'm going to tell you?" He snorted. "You must be younger and more naïve than you sound, Xi. Guild members don't share that kind of information."

"They do if they want to stay alive."

Straightening in the chair, he ground his teeth. "Are you truly threatening me? Not very smart, Xi. I suggest you apologize and stop wasting my time before I decide to hunt a very different—"

Someone knocked on the door.

Three slow, firm knocks.

"Little K, little K," cold threat laced Xi's laugh through the phone connection, "let me in."

Manson slid his stare to the closed motel room door.

"C'mon, old man," Xi said through the phone, laugh turning into a cajoling croon. "Let me in." He paused, the silence drilling into Manson's ear. "Unless you want to the guild to know just how old you *really* are."

3

Amber scrambled to her feet, heart wild. "Who's Kade?"

Handing her back her phone, Kitt frowned at Ray. "My boss," he mumbled. Lifting his gaze to her, he let out a shaky breath.

"Boss?" A cold lump filled her throat. "Who talks to their boss like that?"

In all their increasingly relaxed and addictive conversations over the last six weeks, they'd never talked about his work.

She'd thought he didn't have a job to go to. Of course, secret dire wolf shifters probably had to pay the bills somehow, but she'd never seen him actually walk into any place that looked like it could be a place of employment. Of course, she'd only just amped up her stalking—no no, her *surveillance* of him—around the clock yesterday.

"What *do* you do for a living?" she asked. Seriously, none of this kind of thing was covered by her degree in paleontology.

A weak chuckle bubbled up from his chest, and he

looked at her again. "I work for a protection and security agency called Guarded Souls. Trust me, your brother's going to be safe. I promise. But we have to leave. Now."

She stared at him. Didn't move.

Trust him? He'd punched out her big brother. How could she go *anywhere* with him now?

He's a dire wolf shifter. You freed him from a cage. He saved you from a creepy old guy. And now that creepy old guy should be dead but seems to be alive and is quite possibly after you now because of what you did. What else are you going to do?

"How soon will Nathanial or...who was the other person?"

"James," he mumbled, eyes fluttering closed for a second.

"How soon before Nathanial or James will be here? Are they...as big and scary as you?" Not exactly what she was going to ask, but now was not the time to reveal she knew exactly what he was, and the question, 'Are they not-human like you?' kinda gave it away.

Later. She'd tell him what she knew later. Maybe when she somehow had him tied to a bed or something.

A bed?

A tight lick of something thoroughly inappropriate swiped through her core and she bit the inside of her bottom lip. What was her brain *doing*? Why was she thinking of tying Kitt to a bed? And seriously, was she *really* going to leave her unconscious brother with two strangers who may or may not be human?

If it means he's safe from Manson the creepy old hunter, yes. Yes you are.

"Within the next few minutes," he answered, words almost a slur.

He didn't look good. Not as bad as he had back in the warehouse, but not good.

"And if you're life's under threat," he mumbled, "who better than an angel or a gen..."

He tumbled sideways. Hit the operating table.

She leapt at him, grabbing his arm just as he began to sink to the floor.

"This is getting a bad habit," she complained, working his arm around her shoulders again.

Eyes half-closed, head slumped forward, he slurred something. *Thank you*, maybe. *Sorry*? *Got milk*? She couldn't quite make it out.

Giving Ray one last quick, worried look, she hitched Kitt's arms farther around her shoulder and headed for the door.

Out it.

At least this time, Kitt walked/shuffled along with her.

"Just stay here for a second," she ordered, leaning him against the wall next to the door.

He grunted out a weak laugh, his head wobbling on his shoulders in an equally weak nod. "Give...me a..."

She grabbed the door handle, reached back inside and turned the latch to the auto-lock position, and then pulled the door shut. Stared at it for a second, before digging her phone out of her pocket again.

Heart thumping like a cannon in her temples, she opened her last text conversation with Mick.

Hey, she typed. *Can you check in on Ray, please? He's at his clinic.*

Hitting send, she shoved her phone back into her pocket, and slid her arm around Kitt's back. "C'mon, big guy. Let's get you...somewhere."

He slurred something again—it sounded like *genie*

protect him, but what the hell did *that* mean?—and let her take some of his weight.

She hurried them both to her rental. At least this time he was partly dressed. Her frazzled brain was still trying to process just how wrong it was of her to admire how freaking hot and impressive he was naked. And how hard it had been to *not* watch when Ray had slid the sweatpants she'd packed onto his unconscious form.

Pulse pounding, she deposited him into the front passenger seat this time and helped him put his thick, muscular legs into the car, before buckling him in, closing the door, and running around to the driver's side.

Yanking open the door, she shot Ray's clinic a quick look.

Guilt and worry and fear twisted into a heavy knot in her stomach. Her lips prickled. "Oh boy, Amber," she exhaled. "You better know what you're doing."

She'd never been this impulsive. What paleontologist was? The study of fossils and ancient remains required patience and modulated consideration. Taking risks wasn't her normal playbook. Of course, her normal playbook went out the window the day she discovered an ancient *canis dirus* molar at South Dakota dig that wasn't exactly... normal.

"Oh boy," she mumbled again, dropping into the driver's seat.

Kitt mumbled something back.

Gripping the steering wheel, she gave him a quick frown.

Tiny beads of sweat covered his forehead. Dark shadows smudged the sallow skin under his closed eyes. "You don't look good."

"You...however..." he slurred, lips tugging into an

almost-smile, eyes rolling under his eyelids, "...look gorgeous."

She snorted, and stab the key into the ignition. "You really *are* delirious."

A weak chuckle fell from him. "Let's..."

Her phone burst into life, the sound of Queen Latifah singing about walking dinosaurs filling the car.

"Crap." Twisting behind the wheel, she dug it out of her pocket. Unfamiliar number.

"Nope. I don't have time for this."

Denying the call, she tossed her phone into the center console storage cavity, started the car and floored the accelerator.

The Prius glided out of the carpark, silent and strangely anticlimactic.

Scowling, she merged into the busy traffic. "Wish these rentals had tinted windows," she complained under her breath. If anyone gave the Prius a cursory glance it'd probably look like she was driving around a dead guy.

A hot dead guy, but dead all the—

Her phone rang again. Same number.

"Seriously?" She ignored it. In the seat beside her, Kitt let out a low snore.

She grunted. Snoring was better than nothing.

Her phone fell silent. And started ringing a heartbeat later.

"You're kidding," she snarled, snatching it up and connecting the call with a swipe of her thumb. "What?"

"I want to speak to Kitt," a male voice said on the other end, so thick and smooth it was like the words were liquid velvet pouring into her ear. "Now."

She blinked, and shot Kitt—motionless again save for

his rising and falling chest—a glance. "Who the hell is this?"

"Kade."

A shiver rippled over her, tightening everything. "Kade?" Kitt's boss?

Kitt's eyelids moved, as if he was trying to pry them open. "Tell him...I'm..." His head lolled to the side, his breathing deep and even.

"He's what?" Kade demanded.

"How did you hear that?" Amber asked. *She'd* barely heard the indistinct mumble.

"I have very good hearing," Kade answered. "Please put Kitt on."

Pressing her phone to her chest, she frowned at Kitt. "Kitt?"

He didn't answer her whisper. Once again, the only thing moving on him was his chest. Up and down, up and down.

At least he was breathing.

Returning her phone to her ear, she grimaced. "He's... asleep."

"I can hear that in his breathing. Tell me, whoever you are, what is going on?"

Whoever she was. Well, that was a question she wasn't ready to answer. Not to the mysterious boss-man Kade, that was for certain. Not when she'd spent the last six weeks lying about it to get closer to the sleeping/unconscious man...creature...being...no, *man*—regardless of what he could transform into—on the seat beside her. "I'm a friend of Kitt's."

More lying. Yay.

Although, he had said, or implied, he was going to ask her out before all this happened, so...

Oh my God, Amber. You need to get a grip and—

"I know all of Kitt's friends," Kade replied. "I don't know you."

"All of them? Seriously?"

"Seriously."

This was not going well. Definitely not a part of her playbook. She was driving too fast, with no destination, and a mountain of worry and guilt and fear crushing down on her. Sam Neill and Alan Grant would be even more ashamed.

"I'm his coffee-shop friend," she blurted out.

"Amber?"

She blinked at the smooth murmur of her name. Her heart quicken.

He'd spoken about her. To his work colleagues. A rush of surreal happiness spread through her and a smile stretched her lips. He'd talked about her.

"You're Amber, yes?" Kade said.

The sudden urge to spill everything, who she was, why she was here, what she knew about Kitt, it all rolled through her, built on her tongue...

"What's going on, Amber?" Kade asked.

The impulse turned to a hot and choking need in her mind. As if the very existence of life depended on her telling him everything.

"Tell me," Kade instructed through the phone.

Warm, shaking fingers wrapped around the phone in her hand, brushing against her own fingers, and she let out a yelp, jerking around in the seat to stare at Kitt.

He sat up straighter in the passenger seat, sweat trickling down his temples. But his eyes were clearer. His color less pale. "Let me talk to him," he said, removing the phone from her ear.

She frowned at him, and then yelped again as a car behind her honked its horn.

Shit. The road. Concentrate on the road.

"Kade," Kitt's voice tickled her senses. She forced her attention to stay on the traffic in front of her. Driving in LA was insane, compared to San Francisco. San Francisco was chill and easy and not scary to navigate. Why Ray and Mick still lived here... Weirdos, the pair of them.

They're the weirdos? You're in some kind of real-life action-adventure paranormal movie and you're thinking about local traffic?

And was she the damsel in distress in said adventure, or the plucky fish-out-of-water character? Or the femme fatale...

Oh God, stop it!

"It's okay."

She pulled a breath at Kitt's low growl. He sounded better. Not best, but better. Maybe whatever Ray had done was helping?

"No, I'm okay. We're okay. I'm more worried about her brother, Ray."

A thick lump filled her throat.

"That's good," he responded to whatever Kade said.

"What's good?" She flicked him a glance.

"Nathanial is already at your brother's clinic."

"Whoa. That was quick. Is he—"

Kitt held up a finger, clearly listening to Kade again. He frowned. "A *Monstrum Venator*," he finally said. "But there's something...different about him. Never come up against one like this bastard."

More silence as Kade spoke.

Amber strangled the steering wheel, eyes burning as she stared at the street ahead.

"No," he said. "I want Ray kept safe. Who's available at the moment to take over from Nathanial?"

A beat of silence, and then Kitt chuckled. "That'll be an interesting pairing. Okay, take the fee out of my next— You sure? Thanks, I owe you one."

Another stretch of quiet, long enough to make Amber look at Kitt again.

The frown was back, and he was pinching the bridge of his nose, eyes closed, jaw bunched. "No," he growled this time, shaking his head.

Uh oh. *No* what?

"No. This is personal."

He shook his head at Kade's response. Every muscle in his body seemed to stiffen, as if suddenly coiled to attack. A low gnarl rumbled deep in his chest.

Amber swallowed, mouth dry. Had the interior of the Prius suddenly got smaller?

"I know," he said into the phone, each word modulated. "And I appreciate it, but I need to deal with the bastard myself. I think he's the one who killed Basia."

Amber's breath caught. She shot Kitt a quick look, heart thumping hard up into her throat. Basia? Who was Basia? And who had killed her? Manson?

Oh God, what had she got herself into?

And more to the point, how did she get out of it?

Easy. Pull over, get out of the car, and run away. Get your ass back home to San Francisco. Forget all about dire wolf shifters and getting your article published in the Journal of Vertebrate Paleontology *or* Paleobiology *or* Scientific American. *Just get away from Kitt now.*

Knuckles aching, she stared back out through the windshield.

She could do that. It was the sane thing to do. The safe thing to do. But did she want to?

"Yeah," Kitt said, the growl gone from his voice. "I'll do that. Promise. No, I won't. Yeah, yeah, I will." He let out a tired chuckle. "I'll do my best. Keep you posted."

She locked her stare on the road. Kept it there as he returned her phone to the center consol.

He'll do what? And he won't what? And he will what?

A prickling pressure told her he was studying her.

"You're not going to kill me, are you?" she asked.

He burst out laughing, the surprised sound bouncing around the Prius' quiet interior. "No. Why would you even think that?"

She shrugged, and then let out her own wobbly laugh. "I'm not used to being in this kind of situation, but I get the feeling this is nothing new for you."

"True." A low moan followed the answer, along with the sound of him moving in his seat. "Although the ability not to be able to shift is..."

He trailed off.

Now. Tell him what you know now. Rip it off like a freaking Band-aid.

"Do you feel any better?" she asked, keeping her focus on the tailgate of the Corvette in front of her.

"I'm not dead, so that's a start."

She flicked him a look.

His eyes caught hers, their golden depths direct. Questioning. "Where are we going?"

She blinked, jerked her attention back to the Corvette and shrugged again. "I have no freaking clue."

He laughed again. "You may not be telling me the entire truth about who you are, Amber Calegari, but you're so damn likeable it almost doesn't matter."

Almost.

Throat tight, she shot him another glance.

He held her gaze for a moment, and then settled back into the seat with a wince, closing his eyes as he pointed toward the front of the car. "A motel, Jeeves. Somewhere where we can park the car directly outside the door."

"For a quick getaway?"

"For a quick getaway." The corner of his mouth curled. Why did she want to kiss it so much? "And easier pizza delivery."

She smiled. Couldn't help herself. What else was the plucky heroine with a dark secret meant to do when the dire wolf shifter beside her was also so damn...likeable?

ALRIGHT, so as soon as they were in the motel room, he'd demand answers.

Watching Amber through the passenger window as she hurried up to the Holiday Inn's reception desk, he pressed his palm to his side.

Whatever her brother had done, it was helping.

Somewhat.

Deep inside, his wolf still paced and snarled. Still trapped. Still imprisoned.

He'd tried to shift the second Amber climbed out of the car. Not to run away, or attack, but to just...see if he could.

Nothing. All he'd done was poke the pissed-off dire wolf of his duel existence.

At least the pain from his wound in his side had subsided somewhat. That was something. All he could do now was hope to hell whatever the hunter had shot into him would soon fade away.

Then, when he could shift again...

"Room 42," Amber muttered, dropping into the driver's seat and slamming the door shut. "The ultimate room."

He frowned. "The what?"

Shaking her head, she started the Prius. "Never mind." She put the car into Drive and pulled away from Reception.

He studied her. Kept studying her until she brought the car to a halt—nose first—a few moments later in front of a brightly painted blue door.

"Forty two," he said, reading the number on it.

"Life, the universe, and everything, baby."

"What?"

Letting out a sigh, she shook her head again and opened her door. "Let's get you inside."

She climbed out and hurried around the front of the car, muttering some more under her breath.

Words she probably thought he couldn't hear. Words he *would* have heard more clearly if not for the shit in his system suppressing his *croi*: *Why the hell am I saving a guy who doesn't know anything about Hitch-hiker's Guide to the Galaxy?*

He blinked. Hitch-hiker's guide to the what?

"Here we go," she muttered, opening his door and reaching in for him. "Wrap your arm around...yeah, like that." He tried to support as much of his weight as he could as she helped him out of the seat.

Pain lashed up his side and sank into his shoulder, but not as much as before. He bit back a wince, and straighten his spine.

She was too small, too womanly to be lugging his weight around.

And yet, she's done it over and over since finding you in the cage. Impressive, but why?

It took them only a few moments to get inside the room. His wolf snarled and paced the whole time.

"Shit." She stopped just inside the door. "I asked for a…"

One lone king-sized bed sat in the middle of the room, dressed in a cheery floral-patterned duvet and what looked like a cushion store's entire inventory.

"Doesn't matter." She adjusted her grip on his wrist and began walking towards the bed. "I'm not planning on sleeping here."

"Until I've…neutralized the hunter," he said, fighting to hide the pain in his voice, "you're not going anywhere."

Neutralized. That was one way of saying *rip the throat out of*.

She snorted, and deposited him on the bed's edge. "What if I just run out of this room right now?"

He met her gaze. "I'd chase you down."

Her breath caught.

"Don't be foolish, Am. You know you've found yourself in something you weren't prepared for. And you know your life is now in danger. I can keep you safe. I promise. I just need some rest."

She licked her lips.

"And some answers."

Her shoulders slumped. "Okay."

Pressing his hand to his side, he made himself a little more comfortable, and then indicated she take a seat beside him on the mattress's edge.

Instead, she took a few steps to the small table and chairs beneath the room's window. Dropped into one of the chairs. Studied her thumb nail.

His wolf drew motionless. Tasted the air. Listened to her heartbeat.

It beat faster than normal in her chest. He'd become attune to its rhythm during their moments together in the café. There was something about its steady thump that settled him. He'd found himself looking forward to hearing it, just as much as he looked forward to seeing her, and talking to her.

More than once he'd found himself grinning while getting ready for work of a morning, knowing he was most likely going to bump into her during his caffeine pitstop on the way to the Guarded Souls office.

More than once he'd found himself thinking of her at home, drawing an image of her into his mind while preparing dinner, or folding his laundry. Or standing in the shower...

He pulled a slow breath and fixed his focus completely on her now. "Who are you? Really?"

Her heart beat quickened. She caught her bottom lip with her teeth. Her eyebrows knitted into a frown. And then she lifted her head and met his stare. "I really *am* Amber Calegari," she answered, voice husky. "I promise."

"Okay, So who's Amber Calegari when she's *not* pretending to be a veterinarian?"

A soft, wry laugh fell from her and she rolled her eyes, cheeks growing pink, tiny dimple denting her right cheek. "Umm..."

Hell, he'd never wanted to kiss someone as much in he wanted to kiss her right then.

Right then, it didn't matter she was keeping a secret from him, had in all likely hood deceived him. Right then, he wanted to cup her face in his palms and brush his lips over hers. Like he'd wanted to since the second time they bumped into each other at the coffee house. Probably even the first time.

She'd literally collided with him that first time, coffee in one hand, phone in the other, attention fixed on whatever she'd been typing. Her coffee had splashed out of her keep-cup and she'd gushed out a mortified apology, wiping at the brown stain spreading on his shirt with frantic panic, fingers swiping over his abs and stomach repeatedly before she'd let out a startled *eep* and scurried back a step, wide brown eyes locking with his.

He'd replayed that moment over and over that night, chuckling every time.

The next day, she'd been entering the café as he was leaving it, and melodramatically stepped aside, grinning at him as she waved him past her. "It's safe today," she'd said. "I'm not going to feel you up." She'd smacked her palm to her mouth, eyes growing as wide as they had the day before. "Oh God, did I really just say that?"

Yeah, right then...he'd wanted to kiss her.

That desire only grew every time they saw each other in the café.

By the time he found himself in the karaoke bar with James, struggling with his growing, complicating attraction to her, in his head he already *had* kissed her. That and so much more.

Remembering that first meeting in the café now however...he'd been enamored from the very second she'd touched him. Blinded by her adorability to the fact the way they first met was incredibly cliché. As if the whole moment had come out of corny romantic comedy movie.

Chest tight, inner wolf growling, he leaned an elbow on his knee and pinned her stare with his. "No lies, Am.

Who are you? And why did you make sure we met in the café all those weeks ago?"

Her throat worked as she swallowed. She moistened her lips with a quick swipe of her tongue. Her breasts rose and fell with a long, ragged breath. And then she closed her eyes and shook her head. "I guess if you kill me it'll be my own fault," she muttered.

He narrowed his eyes.

She looked at him again, shoulders slumping. "I'm a paleontologist, Kitt."

"Like Alan Grant? In *Jurassic Park*?"

"I *knew* I liked you for a reason!" she burst out, before slapping her palm to her mouth, eyes darting all over the room. "I mean, yes. Like Alan Grant."

He couldn't help but chuckle, even as a prickling sensation swept over him. Paleontologist. Someone who studied dinosaurs. Or at least, ancient things.

Drawing in another long breath, he regarded her. "So what's so secretive about being a paleontologist that you couldn't tell me that's what you are?"

She met his gaze again, cheeks turning pinker. "I... umm...I specialize in *canis dirus*."

Kitt grew motionless. His inner wolf snarled.

Canis dirus.

Dire wolf.

"I mean," she went on, eyes once again jumping all over the motel room, "paleontologists don't specialize in one particular species, as such. We have subdisciplines— mine's vertebrate paleontology—but some of us tend to get hung up on a particular species. So when we discover fossils *of* that particular plant or animal..." She flicked him a look, and then went back to frowning at her thumbnail. "Well, I'm sure you can imagine. *Canis dirus* has been my main interest since I learned about them at college. I'm very good at recognizing and classifying *canis dirus* fossils."

Blood roaring in his ears, he balled his fists. Waited until she looked back at him. "I see."

She licked her lips again. Her heart pounded like a cannon, hammering at his sensitive hearing.

"Continue." What else could he say? She'd saved him, after all. And he had no clue just how much she knew.

Could she really know anything? Unlikely. What human would believe it, anyway?

So why is she here? How did she know where the Monstrum Venetor *had you caged? Why did she save you?*

"And Amber?" he growled.

"Yes?"

"Don't lie to me."

Nodding her head, she let out a shaky breath. "When new *canis dirus* fossils are found, I usually get called in," she said. "A few months ago a new find was uncovered in the North Bijour Hills, in South Dakota."

North Bijou Hills.

A cold chill rushed over him.

Shit. North Bijou Hills.

Surely she wasn't... She couldn't be.

Staring at her, he clenched his fist tighter. He'd left nothing behind after the fight in the North Bijou Hills with the mountain lion shifter over two hundred years ago. The bastard cat had stumbled upon him when he'd been morning Basia. Had sensed Kitt's weakness and attacked. The fight had been short but brutal. Kitt barely got out of it with his life. Had holed himself up in a nearby cave and licked his wounds for months until he was healed enough to resume human form and walk away.

The mountain lion shifter hadn't walked anywhere ever again.

But that was so long ago. Over two centuries.

She's a paleontologist, remember. She's all about old things.

Forcing his body to relax, he studied her.

"There were so many *canis dirus* fossils there," she went on, meeting his gaze. "As if hundreds of dire wolves had come there to die over a period of a thousand of years." Her eyes grew distant and a small smile curled her lips. "It was fascinating. I'd never found a dig like it. I lost myself there. But one night, when I was working on the dig alone, I found...something else."

He grew still. Raced through his memory of his fight with the mountain lion shifter.

There'd been lots of blood shed and flesh torn. But none of it would have survived the centuries. So what—

Your tooth.

Pulse pounding, his tongue moved to the empty spot on his gum, way back in his mouth, where his second molar would be *if* he hadn't lost it during the fight.

The other shifter had king hit him while he'd been in human form. He'd shifted into wolf form on impact, before his body hit the ground, but his molar...

"A tooth," he said, forcing his voice to be calm, steady.

She stared at him. Didn't move.

"You found a tooth."

"Yes."

Fuck.

"A tooth that wasn't right," she said.

He closed his eyes. Remembered the crunching blow from the shifter. "What was wrong with the tooth?"

The question came out a raspy growl.

The soft sounds of her fidgeting in the chair scraped at

his sanity. Regretting her decisions leading up to this point? Or scared for her life?

Opening his eyes, he looked directly at her.

"It was a *canis dirus* molar," she said. "But it wasn't a fossil. And it wasn't formed correctly. It was like it was half a dire wolf's tooth and half..."

She stopped.

He waited.

He wasn't going to say it. She had to.

"Half human." She licked her lips. "I took it. Didn't tell anyone about it. Which is completely insane and totally out of character for me. But here's the thing; I took it because I know *canis dirus* better than anyone in the country. Anyone. And I *knew* this tooth wasn't just malformed. It was...something different."

"Different?"

She nodded her head, a ferocity about her he'd never seen before. An excitement. "It wasn't a *normal* dire wolf tooth, but what *was* it? I took it, studied it. Tried to extrapolate as much information from it the traditional ways, and then decided to extract any DNA I could from the root canal."

He closed his eyes again.

Fuck.

"My brother—not Ray, Mick—is a forensic detective. I asked him to run a trace on the DNA. I pulled the little sister card. But something told me to see the results before he did, so I fernangled it so I did."

Despite everything, a wry chuckle rumbled up through his chest. "Fernangled?"

"Fernangled. It helps when you can pull the Doctor card, although I suspect a PhD in Paleontology means squat to the lab rats who ran the test. Still, I'm glad I did, despite probably skirting what's legal and what isn't."

Clenching his jaw, he pictured her the first time they met: eyes twinkling with playful embarrassment, lips curling, dark hair a mass of waves tumbling around her face, making him want to comb his fingers through it to see if it was as soft and silky as it appeared. Remembered how she smelt—vanilla and jasmine and coffee all mingled together. Remembered how her laugh made his heart quicken and how that part of his body long since dormant filled with hot interest...

And it seemed all this time, she was hunting him.

His head roared louder. His wolf prowled and gnarled and struggled against the hunter's mysterious concoction crippling it.

"And I think you know why it was good I kept all this to myself," she said. "Don't you."

Chest tight, gut rolling, he opened his eyes and stared at the floor between his bare feet. "Because the DNA was human."

"Because the DNA was human," she confirmed. "And it led me to you."

He lifted his head and found her staring straight at him. Unafraid. "Tell me how that's possible, Kitt?"

His wolf growled. Lashed out. Snarled. And retreated to silence as he pulled a slow breath and willed it to calm down. He couldn't get angry. Not yet. Not until he knew what exactly she hoped to achieve. "How long have you been watching me, Amber?"

A delicate pink touched her cheeks, and she lowered her gaze.

"Before we first crashed into each other at the coffee house?"

Returning her gaze to his, she nodded.

He closed his eyes for a second.

Fuck.

His wolf snarled, threatened. No, not threatened, agitated. Or something else...

Here was a human woman he'd grown to trust, to desire, and as such, his inner wolf had done the same.

When it came to his duality, his human/wolf existence, his inner dire wolf ruled his fight or flight reflex. Protected him. Primal and instinctual, it viewed the world and those in it the way all animals did—what was a threat, and what wasn't? Until now, it had never viewed Amber as a threat.

How did it view her now?

He let his consciousness seep into its. Felt what it felt...

Ah, conflicted. Yeah.

Right here with you on that one, he thought, slipping out of his wolf's mind.

"So, Dr. Calegari," he said, pressing his palm to his side. The wound ached again; a hot, throbbing pulse. "What do you *think* you know?"

Licking her lips once more, she fidgeted on her seat. Her heart hammered fast, its beat pounding against his ears.

"I think..." she began, before stopping, letting out a shaky laugh, and rolling her eyes. "I can't believe I'm actually saying this aloud. For the first time. I'm saying this aloud. Oh boy." She swiped at her mouth, studied him over her palm for a heartbeat, and dropped her hand. "I think, based on the evidence I've collected and seen, you're some kind of paranormal creature who can shift between human form and dire wolf form."

He closed his eyes and dropped his head.

Shit.

4

W hy wasn't he saying anything?

Doing anything?

She'd kind of expected him to deny it. Bark at her. Lunge at her.

Try to kill her.

Okay, she'd hoped he *hadn't* tried to do that, but hey, she'd just told him she knew what he was, and she was pretty certain humans weren't meant to know that.

Or maybe it was common knowledge and she was just out of the loop. She did spend most of her time brushing at the fossilized remains of long-dead animals out in the middle of nowhere after all. And when she wasn't doing that, she was, well, vagueing out as only a nerd can: either by watching movies, reading books, or RBGing.

But then, if it was a widely known thing people like him existed, surely Ray or Mick would have said something at some point. Those two were constantly telling her what to look out for. The last time she'd tried to go on a date—way too many years ago, Mick had driven up to San Francisco and tailed them both. She'd resorted to cornering him in the men's bathroom at the movie complex, giving him a nipple-cripple, and telling him to back the fuck off before he'd finally faded from sight.

So the odds that they'd let her wander around oblivious to this kind of revelation were slim.

Slimmer than slim.

Which suggested people generally didn't know about dire wolf shifters. So why wasn't Kitt reacting to the fact she did?

"Kitt?" Alright, could she sound any more nervous? "Are you...umm...did you hear me?"

He lifted his head, and she gasped at the muted golden glow of his eyes.

"What are you planning to do with what you know, Am?"

Still calling you Am. That's a good sign, right?

She swallowed. Maybe? Maybe he was lulling her into a false sense of security.

"Am?"

Fidgeting on the chair, she lowered her stare to her thumb. "I was going to write a paper on you. Have it published in an international paleontology or scientific journal. Reveal your existence and become famous."

She tensed up, waiting for the attack.

"You were..." His laugh bounced around the room.

Jerking her head up, she frowned at him. "Why are you laughing?"

He shook his head, winced, and rubbed at his bandaged side. "This is not helping, you know."

She gaped, even as a part of her noted how freaking sexy his eyes were when they glowed. "*Why* are you laughing? I thought you'd be furious. I thought you'd try to kill me."

Wincing again, he pressed at his side some more and held up his other hand, index finger raised. "Wait."

Huffing into the strands of her hair escaped from her braid, she folded her arms and glowered at him. "I don't understand what's going on," she grumbled.

She hated not understanding what was going on. Not when it came to dire wolves, at least. It offended her.

He chuckled, explored his side with his hand again, and shook his head. "I've been hunted most of my existence, but this is the first time the hunter didn't want to kill me, or keep me as a pet."

"A pet?"

He snorted. "Long story. One day you can ask Kade about it. No, actually better you don't. It's still a sore spot with him. Ask Christen."

"Who?" Her head spun. She'd been ready to...to...fight for her life? Maybe? Plead for it? Promise him anything? Ready for *something*, at least, but not Kitt laughing as if she'd just told him a—

"Wait," she said, sitting up straight. "Do you think I'm joking?" How dare he. "I'm not joking. I know what you are. I have photos. Videos." She paused. Chewed her lip. "Okay, so I don't actually have photos or video of you changing yet, but I saw it happen. With my own eyes. Well, I didn't. I saw you in human form and then a split second later you were in dire wolf form, but I bet it's amazing to watch. *And* I was going to..."

She stopped again.

He arched an eyebrow at her, that beautiful, ethereal light in his eyes slowly fading until he appeared completely normal again. "What? Catch me? Cage me up? Make me shift form so you could capture it on film?"

The words left him on a calm, relaxed murmur.

"Umm..." She fidgeted on the seat again. "Well...no. Not exactly. I was just going to stalk you until I was lucky enough... I mean, despite looking like I've got this planned out, I've been kind of making it up as I went along these last few days."

"You realize you're not Indiana Jones, right?"

Throwing up her hands, she slumped back against the chair. "Why does everyone keep insisting I think I'm Indiana Jones? He's an archeologist, not a paleontologist."

A small smile tugged at Kitt's lips. "Sorry."

She glared at him. And then let out a sigh. "Okay, so *you* know *I* know. And now you know *what* I was going to do with that knowledge. What are you going to do about it?"

He studied her, motionless. And then shrugged. "I'll think about it after I deal with the *Monstrum Venator*."

"The old dude who should be dead, yes? Manson?" An image of the thin, elderly man back in the warehouse filled her head. His threat to feed her to Kitt wormed its way back into her brain. A cold lump rolled over in her stomach.

"The old dude," Kitt confirmed, closing his eyes again. Pain etched his face. He may not be barely conscious any more, but he was still clearly hurting. Was that why he'd responded to her confession with a laugh. If he'd been uninjured, would he have ripped her apart?

If he was uninjured, you'd still probably be chasing him around in stalker mode.

For all her bravado and brains, she really hadn't thought any of this through. Not really.

Stalking a massive man who could shape-shift into an equally massive, prehistoric wolf with the intention of revealing what would no doubt be a fairly sizable secret for him? Yeah, not overly smart, when it came down to it. "He spoke of some guild. Will more come after you now?"

"Us." He opened his eyes, the glow back in their golden depths again. "You'll be just as much a target as I am now. But no. *Monstrum Venator* don't work together. They're solo hunters. In fact, apart from bragging about their kills, they usually avoid each other."

"Okay, so only one old creepy guy coming after...us." The cold lump in her stomach twisted at the thought. "That's something, I guess."

He chuckled. Winced. Touched his side again. "Something."

"You need to rest," she admonished, rising to her feet and crossing to the bed. "Heal."

Lowering herself to sit beside him, she gently removed his hand from the bandaging.

"I just need to not move for a while," he said, voice low and scratchy. "I've been dragged around a bit since getting out of the bastard's cage."

Lifting an eyebrow at him, she fought to stop her lips twitching. "Are you dissing my saving techniques?"

He let out a weak chuckle, and then a slow breath as she touched her shaky fingers to the pristine white square of sterilized gauze taped over his wound. "Never," he mumbled.

She smiled, lowering her attention to his side.

She'd never been able to handle the sight of blood. For a while—as a young teenager—she'd considered following in Ray's sizable footsteps and go to college to become a vet, but realized after only one day volunteering at the local clinic she didn't have the stomach for it. Paleontology however? Not a drop of blood to be found. Not fresh blood, at least.

Standing on the other side of the operating table as Ray had dug out the bullet in Kitt's side, cleaned the wound, and stitched it closed...well, she'd almost thrown up. The only way she'd got through it was to hold Kitt's hand and comb her fingers through his hair. Calm herself as she calmed him—although to be fair, he was completely unconscious at the time, as well as dosed up with something Ray had given him, so he was already pretty calm. Her hand holding and hair stroking hadn't really helped him at all.

Her, though? It'd definitely helped her.

"It's a good sign there's *no* sign of blood," she said now, trailing her fingers over the medical tape pulling at his smooth skin. "It means it's not bleeding through. The stitches are holding."

She frowned as her fingers moved back to the bandaging. How could a man who turned into a wolf be so smooth? Where did all the fur go?

Does it matter? Seriously? Have you ever seen muscle tone and definition like this? Where does the fur *go? Where does all that exquisite human physiology go, more like it.*

"Your brother did good."

She lifted her head at Kitt's low murmur.

His eyes glowed warm light. His pupils...

Not quite human. Not quite canis dirus.

Oh wow. Wow.

"When this is over," he went on, motionless, holding her gaze with his incredible eyes, "I'd like to repay him for his help. I've got a friend who's a master at granting wishes. I'll get James to—"

She kissed him.

Leaned toward him, brushed her lips over his, the way she'd wanted to from their first conversation all those weeks ago, and kissed him. The way she'd dreamed of doing every time they had coffee together at the café.

So many times during those moments she'd forgotten *what* he was, *why* she'd orchestrated their meeting. When they were sitting together, chatting, she'd forgotten everything except how much fun she was having in his company. And how much she'd like to—

She pulled away, stare locking with his. What the hell was she doing?

"I'm sorry." Jolting to her feet, she rubbed her palms on her thighs and darted her gaze over the floor. "I...I don't know why I did that."

He didn't say anything.

Tossing him a quick look, she shrugged. "Indiana Jones always kisses the damsel in distress he's just saved, right?"

The golden light in his eyes faded. His jaw clenched.

Oh God, so not the right way to proceed.

"I mean," she went on, hugging her elbows, "I'm not saying *you're* a damsel, but you *are* in distress, and I *did* save you, and I'm going to shut up now and go to the ice-machine and pretend this didn't happen, okay?"

She turned for the door, and gasped when a large, firm hand wrapped her wrist, spinning back to him.

He towered over her. He always had. Large and daunting and impressive and so damn...sexy she didn't know how to think, how to breathe.

His gaze held hers, his eyes direct and unreadable and entirely human, before dropping to her lips. Studying them. His pupils dilated. His nostrils flared. "Am..." he murmured.

His grip tightened around her wrist and she swayed toward him. Swayed. Actually swayed. Like a girl craving for more.

Yes. Please. Oh please.

With a low growl, he released his grip and lowered himself back to the side of the bed. "Don't leave this room, Dr. Calegari. I need to rest, but you can't leave this room. It's not safe. Do you understand?"

He looked up at her.

Throat thick, face burning, she nodded. "Yes."

"As soon as I've recovered, I'll deal with the *Monstrum Venator*, but until then you're in danger." Palm to his side, he swung his legs up onto the bed and stretched out flat on his back. The springs groaned. His feet hung over the end. He winced, eyebrows tugging with discomfort, and threaded his fingers together on top of his broad bare chest. "Just...give me a few moments to rest, okay?"

"Okay."

Closing his eyes, he let out a long, slow breath. "Just a few moments," he murmured.

A few seconds later his soft snores buzzed through the room's silence.

Smile pulling at her lips, Amber snorted and picked up the TV remote. She'd never bought a movie from the pay-per-view menu in a motel before. Now clearly was the time to do so.

Scrolling through the catalogue, she made her selection. Of course if the latest *Star Wars* movie was on offer she would take it, even if it cost more than it had to see it at the cinema. Who wouldn't? Well, no one she wanted to hang out with.

She slid Kitt a glance. During their third "accidental" interaction, he'd made a passing *Star Wars* reference ("Punch it, Wookie," he'd said, when he'd handed over his credit card to the cashier). She'd bit the inside of her mouth to stop her excited giggle. Reminded herself she wasn't interested in him for romantic reasons, but scientific ones.

He snorted a little in his sleep, scratched at his chest—still bare and smooth and incredible to run her gaze over—and she smiled again.

And then gasped as someone walked passed their room.

Heart smashing into her throat, she sat motionless as the shadow crossed the curtain and disappeared.

Could the hunter, the *Monstrum Venator*, find them here? Could he find them at all?

Could he actually still be alive? How was that possible?

You're sitting in a motel room with a man who changes into a dire wolf. Anything is possible.

Wriggling on the hard seat, she turned her attention back to the TV.

Stared blankly at the screen.

Yawned.

Wriggled on the seat again.

Pushed herself from it and wandered to the bathroom. Tiny. Clean.

She picked up the complimentary shampoo bottle and admired it. Opened it and took a sniff of its contents.

"Nice," she muttered, twisting the lid back on.

Turning to the mirror, she frowned at her reflection. God, she looked...tired.

You've been awake for over twenty four hours. What did you expect?

"Hmm." She rubbed at her eyes, frowned more, unbraided her hair and attempted to make it look spectacular with her fingers.

"Yeah, that's not going to work." Rolling her eyes, she

worked the crimped mess into one long braid again. Who the hell was she trying to impress, anyway?

The hot paranormal male asleep on the bed? The one you unexpectedly kissed. The one you've failed repeatedly to not imagine taking you in his arms and—

"And that's enough of that," she mumbled, hurrying from the room.

Kitt still slept. On the TV an X-Wing sped through star-speckled space.

She crossed to the window, pulled the curtain aside a fraction and peaked outside.

No movement. Just a bright, hot afternoon, parked cars, and blue blue sky.

She yawned again.

Maybe she should call Mick? Find out how Ray is?

And then he'd demand to know where you are, and are you really ready for that argument?

"Watch the movie, Amber." She dropped back onto the seat.

And threw herself from it. If she sat still for too long, she'd fall asleep in the thing and hurt her neck. No way was she risking that. Not while she was on the run from a possibly zombiefied monster hunter.

Biting at her lip to stop another yawn, she looked at the expanse of untouched bed beside Kitt.

It looked so soft.

What are you thinking? Stop—

Kitt groaned. Low and raw and almost inaudible. "Am…"

Heart catching, she hurried over to him.

Pain twisted his face. His eyes scrunched tighter closed, one hand fisting at his bandaged side, the other flailing open, as if trying to reach for something.

"I'm here," she whispered, snagging his hand and threading her fingers through his. "It's all good. I'm here."

He groaned again, fingers clenching hers, pain etching his face, and then the groan became a growl. A wolf's growl.

"I'm here, Kitt." Heart pounding, she perched on the edge of the bed, her hip nudging his. "I'm here."

The gnarl deepened, grew lower. Lower.

Gone.

Silence again.

Throat thick, she waited.

His grip around her fingers softened; his breathing returned to normal.

"I'm here," she repeated, keeping her voice quiet and calm, not knowing what else to say. Or do. "We're okay."

"Am..." he murmured, before falling silent again.

She brushed a strand of damp hair from his forehead and, letting out a wobbly breath, worked her butt a little further onto the mattress and turned her attention back to the TV.

There was still over half the movie to watch and she wasn't planning on going anywhere.

"I'm here," she whispered again, stroking Kitt's forehead with the tips of her fingers. "We're going to be okay."

God, she hoped she wasn't lying.

XI PROWLED THE ROOM. Picked things up. Turned them over in his large hands. Studied them. Returned them to their spot.

The gun he'd greeted Manson with was now tucked

into his waistband at his back. Manson's dagger had joined it.

Manson hadn't agreed to that redistribution of weapons but XI had been...rather insistent.

Manson touched the tip of his tongue to the fresh split in his lip, cringing at the taste of copper he encountered. "What kind of person punches an old man?"

XI plucked the heavy glass ashtray from the room's small table and jiggled it in his right hand. "You're an old man, just like I'm a law-abiding citizen." He chortled. And then threw back his head and laughed. "Get it?"

Manson narrowed his eyes. "No."

Snorting, XI wandered over to him, ashtray still in hand. "So tell me, old man, why did you think you could use magic and get away with it? Were you originally an *Extraho Venator*?"

"A dragon hunter?" Curling his lip, Manson shook his head. The thought of being a member of *that* ancient off-shoot of the Guild twisted his gut. *Extraho Venator* had no poise, no class, and no subtly. Killing dragon shifters didn't require any. You tracked a dragon, you killed a dragon. Simple.

Extraho Venators also had no real code: whatever means necessary, that was it.

They killed their fellow hunters regularly, used magic indiscriminately, and rumor had it, had no compunction killing any human that got in the way of their hunt.

Rumor had it the Guild were considering excommunicating them.

Couldn't happen soon enough, as far as Manson was concerned. To be accused of being an *Extraho venator*? His gut twisted again, and he glared at XI. "Perhaps I should be asking you the same thing?"

X1 stopped directly in front of him, eyebrows shooting up as he looked down at him. "The thought of using magic turns my stomach, old man."

"I'm not referring to magic," Manson sneered, shaking his hands. The handcuffs locking his arms around the back of the chair X1 had forced him into clanked and clattered; cold steel on cheap plastic.

X1 chuckled, bouncing the ashtray on his palm again. "Ah, that." He shrugged. "I'm not an idiot, K5. You look like you belong in a Norman Rockwell painting, but you caught...something big. And you're using magic of some kind. What else do you suggest I do?"

"If you uncuff me, I'll tell you what that *big* thing is."

Sour bile filled his mouth at the thought of negotiating his freedom with X1, but if it meant getting the cuffs off...

He couldn't retrieve the hypodermic needle he'd hidden under one of the pillows before answering the door while cuffed, but if he could just get to it X1 would be regretting his arrogant actions.

Manson jangled the cuffs against the back of the chair again, eyebrows raised as he looked up at the other hunter.

X1 studied the ashtray for a moment, holding it up so the light in the room glinted off its grimy glass surface, and then swung it down in a sudden arc, smashing it into Manson's cheek.

Manson hit the floor, chair and all. Something snapped in his shoulder, white-hot pain shot down his bound arm, and then a fire replaced it, burning and throbbing.

"You fucking bastard," he wailed, thrashing against the floor, the chair, his broken shoulder.

"Such language for an elderly gentleman," X1 mocked,

clamping a hand around Manson's upper arm and yanking him upright again.

Pain jarred through Manson, but he bit back his cry, glaring instead at Xi as the smug man righted the seat.

"Now," Xi brushed the back of his fingers over Manson's broken shoulder, "let's try that again." He planted the ball of his booted foot on the seat between Manson's thighs, rested his elbow on his raised knee, and —ashtray dangling loosely in his grip—smiled. "What did you capture, and where is it now?"

Manson smiled back. "Or what? Or you'll expose me to the guild? You don't think I've been around long enough to be prepared for such a threat?"

Xi narrowed his eyes. And smashed the ashtray into Manson's cheek again.

The world went black. His shoulder screamed. His cheek did the same.

"Or I'll hurt you," Xi said. He grinned, leaning closer to Manson. "A lot."

Manson spat at him. It wouldn't help get the cuffs off, but it was satisfying, nonetheless.

Xi laughed. "You're a feisty old bastard, I'll give you that." He wiped the wad of blood-tinged spittle from his chin. "And a smart one. I've been researching you long enough to know that. Smart enough to know what you're doing now is futile. Unless..." he narrowed his eyes, "...you have a plan."

He pushed off the seat, the force toppling it and Manson backward.

Fresh pain detonated in Manson's shoulder as the back of the chair smacked into the floor. He cried out before he could stop himself, blurry vision sliding over the ceiling.

"Where is it?" Xi's voice wafted over to him.

"Where's what?" Manson shot back. Mashed beneath the back of the chair and the floor, his hands throbbed. Burned. Had one of his wrists snapped? He couldn't feel his fingers any more. How was he meant to use the clapper in the warehouse if he couldn't use his hands anymore?

Maybe, if your wrist is snapped, you can get your hand—

"Whatever it is you think you're going to take me down with when I let you out of those cuffs," Xi said. The sounds of him moving around the room scraped at Manson's control. "Another knife? I like the first one I took from you. It looks ancient and special."

"It's a *Dáinsleif* blade," Manson said, testing his wrist. Was he moving his hand? He couldn't tell. Maybe?

"Huh." Xi's voice came from further away. "No idea what that means. Should I be impressed?"

Manson suppressed a grunt. Imbecile.

"Ah, what's this?" Triumph danced through Xi's question.

A cold lump settled in Manson's gut, pressed against the base of his spine. He grew motionless, staring at the ceiling. Waited.

Footfalls vibrated through the floor and then Xi grabbed a fistful of his shirt front and yanked him—and the damn plastic seat—upright. Slammed the chair's feet on the floor. Grinned down at him.

Holding up the needle between their faces, he arched an eyebrow. "What's in this?"

Manson swallowed. His shoulder burned. His hands did the same. Were his fingers broken? His wrist?

Xi planted his foot on the seat again, turning his attention to the syringe. "What would this do to me, K? If you injected it into me?"

Mouth dry, Manson stared at the syringe.

Letting out a low laugh, Xı nodded. "Thought as much. So, let's try this again, shall we? Tell me what you caught and where it is now, or I'll inject whatever this is into you."

"A dire wolf shifter."

Between keeping the wolf to himself and his internal organs slowly, painfully dissolving there was no real choice.

Xı's eyebrows shot up. "You're kidding me. I thought they were extinct? I heard the last one was killed by one of the guild over two hundred years ago."

Manson shook his head, stare still locked on the needle. "That was me. I killed the bitch. I thought she was the last of her kind, but I discovered one lone male a few months ago. Have been hunting it ever since. I caught it, caged it, last night. Immobilized it."

"Immobilized it?"

"Yes."

"In the warehouse?"

"Yes." Manson's eyes burned, but he wouldn't blink. Not while Xı held the syringe so close. "I'd planned to contact you about it."

"Planned to gloat?"

"Of course. But some woman broke into the warehouse and freed the thing."

Xı frowned, sliding his attention from the needle to Manson. "A woman? Another guild member?"

"No. But she *was* human."

"And you're sure how?"

"Gut instinct."

Xı didn't question that. There was no need. To be accepted into the Guild, a hunter had to demonstrate a preternatural intuition ability. When it came to gut instinct, a *Monstum Venator*'s was spot on.

"So you're telling me a human female overpowered you and freed the shifter?" XI returned his attention to the syringe. "Maybe you're not as good as I believed. Or as good as you sell yourself. Have you been telling tall tales, K?" He flicked Manson a look and gave the chair a bit of a shake with his foot. "Or maybe your magic isn't keeping you as young as it used to?"

Grinding his teeth, Manson tested the cuffs again. Agony exploded in his wrist and ripped up his arm, but that was it. No movement, no hint he could slip his hands through the metal rings. Getting out of the damn things wasn't possible. Not unless he wanted to de-glove himself.

"She took me by surprise," he confessed. Perhaps, if he played his cards right, he could entice XI to deal with the woman for him. "The wolf had my attention and she attacked me. Despite the fact she's not very big, she's aggressive and fierce."

"She must be." Contempt laced XI's voice.

Manson sneered. "She mocked the guild, X. Ridiculed it. Talked of secret handshakes."

Not exactly the truth, but would it do the job?

A muscle knotted in XI's jaw. "Did she now? So she's not a *Venator* of any order, but is happy to ridicule and poach from us?"

Smiling, Manson nodded. Seed, sown. "Poached is exactly it. Whoever she was, she waited for me to complete a successful hunt and then took the prize without any hard work."

He didn't mention the dire wolf's behavior-- the unexpected moments of strength and resistance to the serum, the sudden and unnerving resurrection from almost death to protect the female, XI didn't need to know any of that. Knowing that would make the other hunter all the more determined to hunt the wolf, and that wasn't acceptable. The dire wolf was Manson's. No one else's.

What he needed was Xi to become fixated on the incredulous and challenging actions of the unknown woman. What he needed was Xi to see *her* as a more worthy hunt than the wolf.

He leaned forward, dropping his voice to a low whisper. Encouraging Xi to lean closer. ""When I find her I plan to turn her into a vampire."

Xi's eyebrows rose again. "A what?"

"Vampire." He poured all his glee into his voice, even as his heart thumped faster. "I'll transform her, release her on dusk in the Angeles National Forest, and hunt her. That way, I'm not breaking the guild's rules of not hunting humans, but I'm making her pay for encroaching and poaching on a guild hunt."

"You can do that?" Surprise laced Xi's question. And contemplation. "Change a human into a vampire?"

Manson suppressed a smirk. He had him hooked. Good.

"Yes," he said with a nod. "A simple little procedure involving vampire blood and an extracted fang. Both of which I have. Imagine the thrill of hunting a newly changed, ravenous vampire?"

Xi slid his tongue over his bottom lip.

"It's been a long time since I hunted a new vampire," Manson went on, dangling the carrot even more. "There's not many of them around these days. I've missed their speed and savagery. I will take her deep into the forest, release her and then the fun begins."

"So turn a human female vampire? And then hunt it?"

Manson frowned. "Yes."

"Are you sure she's not a *Monstrum Venator*?" Xı asked. "Perhaps she's fooled you?"

"No." How dare he? "Yes, she took me by surprise, but no *Monstrum Venator* would behave the way she did. She guarded the wolf's body like it was precious to her, and I don't mean as a trophy. And when I confronted her, she babbled on like she'd never faced any kind of threat before. Definitely not the actions of a guild member, even one trying to poach a kill. And she was scared. I could see it in her eyes."

Xı's eyes narrowed.

Damn it, he shouldn't have said she was scared. He'd just finished painting her as a ferocious prize worth hunting, not a frightened little girlie.

"And she gave me her name," he said, lifting his eyebrows. "No guild member would share that with another, regardless of the situation. You know that, as well as I. It's against the code and against the rules."

Expression unreadable, Xı leaned closer to him. "She gave you her name?"

"Yes. Amber. She said it was Amber, but what kind of fool gives out their real name?"

"No last name?"

"No. Just Amber."

"Describe her to me," Xı ordered on a whispered.

What did he do? He could describe her incorrectly, but on discovering the deception Xı would expose him to the guild. Expose him, or kill him.

"Maybe five foot three," he said, each word slow. Hesitant. "Dark hair pulled back in a long braid. Dark eyes. She wore camouflage gear. Didn't carry any weapons that I could see. Had a very slight accent of some kind."

Xı studied him.

Throat tight, Manson swallowed. "You could hunt her with me." Whatever was going on, he needed to bring it back under his control. "In fact, I'll teach you the procedure to change her. It's simple and very satis—"

XI moved. Fast.

Something stung the side of Manson's neck, something tiny and icy and sharp, and XI loomed directly in front of him, enigmatic eyes holding his, fisting a handful of Manson's hair in a brutal grip.

"Right now, old man," XI murmured, "I've got two option. I can sepress the plunger of the needle in your neck, or let you convince me to keep you alive. I'm still thinking of which one to do." He drew closer, lips curling. "I guess the question is, how can you help me decided?"

...THE CAGE SURROUNDED HIM, closed in on him. Loud clapping shattered his eardrums—crack crack crack—flooding the darkness with bright light and then—crack crack crack—plunging it into darkness. He paced the cage, growling at the shape moving around on the other side of the bars. Let me out, he screamed, blood erupting from his side.

A laugh rose in the darkness, low and male. No, high and female. Caught you, a voice gloated from the darkness—crack crack crack—he winced at the light attacked his eyes. Tried to see the shape, the owner of the voice. Hands clapped again— crack crack crack—and everything went black, except the blood rising around his ankles, his knees, flowing through the silver bars.

Caught you, the voice called again.

He grabbed at the bars, howled, and his fingers slipped from the burning silver, his paws splashing into the river of blood rushing around his legs, soaking into his fur—crack crack crack—*she stood on the other side of the cage, worry eating up her beautiful face.*

I'm sorry, Kitt, *she said,* I don't know how—*crack crack crack*—to kill you, *the voice roared from the blackness.* And nothing can stop me. Gut you, mount your head on my wall, and then—*crack crack crack*—I'll try, *Amber whispered, running toward the cage.* But I don't know how.

She stopped at the bars, staring in at him. You're not human? *Fear twisted her face.* You're a monster? Oh God, you're—*crack crack crack*—in my way, *the voice snarled*—crack crack crack—*as the shape swung the dagger and plunged it into Amber's side.*

No, *he threw himself at the bars, blood splattering from his fur, his muzzle smashing against the cold metal.* No! *His stare locked on Amber's and she slid down, into the ocean of blood and*—

Where the fuck are you?

He swung his head around, clawing at his hair with his hands. Daku?

Your dreams are fucked up, mate, *the dreamwalker's dry voice blew through the warehouse.*

Dreams? *He clawed at his hair again, turning around. Darkness. A cage. Silver bars. Where was Dak? If this was a dream, where was the dreamwalker?* This is a—

Dream. How else would I be here? *Daku walked up to him from nowhere.* I've been waiting for you to dream. We're all worried about you, mate. I wanted to make sure you're okay, but if your dreams are anything to go by, you're not okay. Do you want—

Gut you and skin you and—*crack crack crack*—the hunter raised his dagger and pointed its tip at Amber's body. You did this, wolf. You killed her.

No you didn't, Kitt. *Dak stepped in front of the* Monstrum Venator. *It's a dream. I can help you control it, but you have to—*

—crack crack crack—<u>Kitt</u>, *Amber cried, as the hunter yanked her head back and pressed the dagger to her throat.* Kitt, don't let him kill me don't let him—*the hunter plunged the blade into her neck and—*

Kitt, *Dak appeared in front of him, black eyes drilling into his,* I'm going to take control now. I'm going to—

The Monstrum Venator's *blade burst through Dak's chest and Kitt screamed as every fiber in his body tore apart and his wolf—*

—jolted awake.

Gasping, sweating, Kitt lurched upright.

And let out a long, choppy breath as his brain registered the motel room's interior.

Dream. Just a dream. Dak was right. It was just a dream. When he saw him next, he'd buy him a beer...or get James to 'procure' whatever the dreamwalker wanted.

He released another breath, fighting to steady his rapid heartrate. On the TV screen, the end credits of what was clearly a movie scrolled upward on the screen, the faint music accompanying them epic and familiar. A low chuckle rumbled deep in his chest and he smiled. Amber been watching the latest Star Wars movie while he slept. Where was she now? In the bath—

The mattress shifted a little beneath his butt and he lowered his stare to the bed.

Amber lay stretched out on her side, eyes closed, hands tucked under her cheek, breath deep and regular and slow.

A rush of happiness swept through him, even as an

image of the hunter sinking his knife into her neck flashed through his head.

What a fucked-up dream. He really owed Dak a beer for pulling him from it.

Pushing the memory of the nightmare aside, he ran his gaze over Amber's sleeping form.

She'd removed the over-sized camo jacket, and his body stirred at the sight of her small frame wrapped in a snug black tank top. So fragile and yet, so fierce and feminine.

He swallowed, a heat building deep in his core as he moved his gaze lower down her body.

At some point, she'd kicked off her boots and a fresh wave of joy rolled over him at the sight of her electric-blue toenail polish. Feminine, fierce, fragile and uncon-ventional.

Hell, he liked that.

She lied to you. Remember that. Planned to expose you to the world. You can't forgive her for that, regardless of the color of her toenails.

Swallowing again, he returned his attention to her face.

Her hair was out of its braid, a tousled mess of dark crimpy waves that spilled out around her head on the mattress.

How many times had he wondered what her hair would feel like when they had coffee together? What would it feel like between his fingers now? If he touched it, would she wake up?

Don't. You're already walking a dangerous line. You want her, on a purely physical level. That's bad enough especially after what she did, but being emotionally engaged?

He dropped his stare to her lips. They'd been so soft, so warm, so gentle and shy against his. How the hell had he resisted the need to haul her to his body, to take full possession of her mouth with his? It had roared through him, and he'd almost succumbed.

Had almost snagged her braid in a firm fist and crushed her mouth with the kiss he'd been craving to give her for weeks.

She let out a soft moan in her sleep, barely a breath, and wriggled a little on the mattress, her face twisting into a small frown as she moaned again.

Guilt ribboned through his pleasure. Sure, she'd thrust herself into his dangerous world without knowing it, but if he'd been able to remove the threat of the hunter instead of a fucking half-assed job, she'd be safe now.

He'd failed Basia, failed to protect the prickly female dire wolf shifter. He wouldn't fail to protect the feisty female human.

Amber whimpered, knees drawing closer up to her body, her eyelids creasing as she scrunched up her face again.

Kitt's chest tightened. Whatever she was dreaming about, it wasn't fun. If he could contact Dak, he'd ask him to take care of the situation.

Yeah, like that would go down well: Hi Amber, it looked like you were having a bad dream so I ask a dreamwalker I know to slide into your dream and calm it down for you. No no, I'm sure he didn't poke around in your inner-most thoughts while he was there.

Releasing a sigh, Kitt laid down again and threaded his fingers behind his head, studying the faint cracks in the ceiling. Dak wouldn't go poking about in Amber's thoughts. The dreamwalker was a mysterious one, but he was trustworthy. When it came to the Guarded Souls team, each knew one-hundred percent the others had their back.

Amber moaned again, louder this time, and twitched beside him.

He had to do something. She'd saved him from the hunter, put her life at risk. The least he could do was save her from a bad dream.

Adjusting his body onto his side, he propped his head on his palm and gently placed his other hand on her shoulder. "Shh, Am," he soothed.

And then stopped.

Side. He was lying on his side.

His left side. The one the *Monstrum Venator* had torn open with a bullet full of—

Deep inside, his wolf growled.

Flexed.

A tingle rushed over Kitt. A million pin-pricks of ancient magic as his *croi* began to activate. As his body began to prepare itself for the shift from human form to dire wolf...

Sucking in a sharp breath, he pulled his hand from Amber's shoulder and flattened himself onto his back.

The shift. He could shift again. Whatever the hunter had done to him, it no longer crippled him. He could transform once more into his dire wolf form.

He could shift!

ut don't fucking shift now, idiot!

"Shit," he muttered, clamping down his inner wolf.

No.

The pricking heat razed his flesh, his muscles, his very existence...

Not now.

...and then subsided. Faded away.

Palm pressed to his eyes, Kitt let out an exasperated groan. Talk about being on a rollercoaster. Can't shift, want to shift; *can* shift, not even close to being the right time *to* shift.

Maybe if he slipped from the room and found a park.

It's daylight outside, idiot.

He shook his head, and swiped his hand down over his face, muffling another chuckle.

"What's so funny?"

A wave of delight rushed through him at Amber's husky mumble and he rolled onto his side again, resting his jaw in his hand to smile at her. "Good...afternoon? I think. Evening?" He let out a wry snort. "I have no idea what time it is."

Gazing up at him, she lifted a hand and brushed a strand of his hair away from his temple. "Does it matter?"

He dropped his eyes to her mouth. "Probably not."

She didn't move. Except to pull in a soft breath through parted lips.

Dragging in his own breath, he pushed himself up into a sitting position. "I feel better," he said, resting his arms on his bent knees as he fixed his focus on the TV screen.

The movie's end-credits crawl had finished, the screen returning to the in-house movie catalogue. Would she watch it again with him, if he asked?

"Define better?" She sat up beside him, her gaze heavy on his profile.

He twisted just enough to look down at his bandaged side and pressed his palm to it. "No pain."

"None?" Surprise filled her voice.

Shaking his head, he smiled at her. "None."

"Hmm." She gently touched the bandage.

He grinned. "Nothing. I can feel you touching it, but that's it."

"That's fantastic." Awe shone in her eyes as she smiled up at him. She didn't asked about his ability to shift, but maybe she wasn't aware he hadn't been able to? What *had* the hunter told her back in the warehouse while he'd been unconscious?

Did she assume he couldn't shift due to being shot, or hadn't she thought about it? Her primary focus since saving him from the cage had been getting him medical attention—even if she had gone the veterinarian option— and then getting them both somewhere unknown.

Perhaps it hadn't registered with her at all his ability to

change form had been restrained. After all, he didn't shift into his dire wolf form every hour. Not even every day.

"It is," he answered, chest tight. Did he tell her?

"Did you want me to take the bandage off?"

"Yes please." Did she need to know? Did it change anything now?

Her gaze held his for a moment, an unreadable light in their brown depths, and then she moved her attention to his side.

Drawing a deep breath, he rested his hand on the top of his head and stared at the TV again as she gently removed the tape and gauze.

"Wow," she murmured once it was completely removed. "Oh wow."

He looked down at his side, just as she brushed her fingertips over his skin.

A ripple of raw sensations shot through him at her touch and his inner wolf stirred, extremely awake and hyper aware.

He swallowed, muscles tensing. Hell, he wanted her.

Wanted to press her to the bed and kiss her and explore her beautiful curves and dips with his hands and lips and—

"Looks good," he said, his voice strained.

She let out a shaky laugh. "Ya think?"

The wound from the bullet's entry and Ray's removal of it was barely visible; now just a thin slash of pale, knotted flesh with a row of neat stitches crossing it.

Soon, if his *croi* truly was restored, his body would heal completely and not even a scar would remain.

"Looks good," he repeated, unsure what else to say.

Feathering her fingers over the skin near the stitches, she shook her head. "It's incredible." She caressed his skin with tender strokes, her breath fanning his side as she looked closer at what was left of his injury.

His groin tightened. His blood ran hot. Fast. Deep in his duel existence, his wolf gnarled. Eager.

Did she know what she was doing to him? Did she mean to?

She manipulated you once before.

She had, but was she now? And if so, why?

Because she wants you? As much as you want her?

Heart pounding, he lowering his arm and caught her wrist in a loose but steady hold, stilling her hand. "Am..."

If she kept touching him, he wouldn't be able to control himself.

He had to. Control himself, control his inner wolf.

"Sorry," she murmured, pulling her hand free and straightening from the bed, head down, cheek glowing pink. "I didn't mean..."

A thick rope wrapped his heart at her sudden departure. His wolf growl. *Go after her. Go...*

"I'm just..." Without looking at him, she hurried into the room's small bathroom and closed the door.

Forcing himself to stay on the bed, he sucked in a long breath, and held it as he turned his attention to his side again.

The stitches pierced his flesh, the skin around the tiny entry points healthy. If he had a sharp knife, a blade of some sort, he'd remove them. They weren't necessary any more. "Thanks, Ray," he mumbled with a smile, flopping back onto the mattress. "I owe you."

He'd definitely get James to grant the guy a wish. Without Ray knowing what he was doing, of course. Amber may have been exposed to the non-human paranormal world, but as far as he knew Ray was still unaware.

He frowned, trying to remember every second of being at the veterinarian's clinic. He hadn't shifted—that had been impossible—but had he done anything else, said anything?

"What a fucking mess," he muttered, pushing himself off the bed.

He explored the small room. Opened the mini-fridge. Studied its contents. His stomach growled, reminding him he hadn't put anything in it since the previous morning. A coffee. That James had interrupted, if he had his timeline correct.

Did he? Hell, it had all been a chaotic whirlwind from the minute Kade had sent him and James a text while they'd been at the karaoke bar.

Reaching into the fridge, he snagged a bottle of cola. Sure, he could run to the nearest gas station or convenience store and get one cheaper, but—

With what?

He snorted, straightening from the fridge and opening the bottle. True. All he had on him were a pair of sweatpants. And he had no clue where they'd come from.

"Are you sure you should be on your feet?"

He turned at Amber's soft question, and his breath caught in his throat.

She'd clearly attempted to tidy herself up in the bathroom, her long dark tangle of hair constrained once again in a thick braid that hung now over her right shoulder, its curled end brushing the tip of her breast. Tiny beads of water clung to her eyebrows and eyelashes, and her cheeks appeared flushed but brighter.

Had she splashed water on her face? The quick equivalent of a cold shower?

"I'm okay," he answered. Giving her what he hoped was

a silly grin, he jumped up and down on the spot three times. "See?"

Rolling her eyes, she walked back to the bed and dropped down onto its side. He started to join her, and stopped, sitting himself down at the room's small table instead.

Her scent already played havoc with his senses, his control. Being closer to her wasn't wise.

His wolf rumbled, impatient. For release? Or for Amber?

"So," he said, turning the cola bottle around in his hands. If he focused on the cold hard surface pressing against his fingers, maybe he could tune out her scent, the sound of her heart, the soft whisper of her breath... "Do you come here often?"

She closed her eyes, and palmed her face. "That was lame," she laughed.

"I've never been good with small talk," he admitted.

A smile curled her lips and she met his gaze. "I loved our small talk at the café."

An invisible band wrapped around his chest and he pulled in another breath, tasting her on the air.

Damn it.

"Tell me about how I found your tooth at the dig in North Bijou Hills," she said, settling into a cross-legged buddha position in the middle of the bed.

"For your paper on me?"

She let out a groan. "Okay okay. Maybe I hadn't considered everything fully, but who knew the life of a dire wolf shifter was so fraught with danger. Now tell me about the tooth."

He chuckled, and then leaned back in the uncomfortable chair, stretching his legs out in front and crossing his ankles. "The dig, as you call it, is—or was—a dire wolf graveyard. For centuries, dire wolves would find their way there in their last days living. Instinctually. Or, as was the case for dire wolf shifters, taken there by their pack if they'd died elsewhere."

"Wow." Her eyes sparkled, her face alive with curiosity. "I mean, seriously, wow. There's a belief elephants do a similar thing with some serious evidence to support such a claim, but I didn't know it was a *canis* behavior as well."

"I don't think contemporary wolves do it. Dire wolves and the common gray wolf alive today...well, we're very different."

She snorted. "A point I've argued about many times. I don't how many times I needed to explain a dire wolf wasn't just a bigger version of a *canis lupis*."

An image of her going toe-to-toe with a man in a white lab coat filled his head, her dark eyes flashing with ferocity, her finger jabbing at the man, her other hand on her hip.

"Why do I think you'd be scary to argue against?" he asked with another grin.

She preened. And then waved her hand. "Keep going. The tooth?"

The tooth.

Dropping his gaze to the bottle of cola, he let out a long breath. "I was there, at the graveyard, mourning the last female of my kind when I was attacked by a mountain lion shifter."

"A what?"

"A mountain lion shifter."

"Mountain lion..." she mouthed, stunned amazement filling her face before a frown pulled at her eyebrows. "Wait. You were there mourning..." She stopped, studying him for a moment. "Was she your...your mate?" The word cracked. "How long ago—"

"No." Shaking his head, he pushed himself from the seat and walked around the small room. "We didn't get on. Major personality clash. This was over two-hundred years ago."

"Two hundred—" She slapped her palm to her mouth, eyes wide as she stared at him.

He gave her a wry smile. "Yes, I'm an old man. Actually, I'm young for a dire wolf shifter. If you had to assign me a human age, it'd probably be in the mid-thirties. Give or take a decade."

Her eyes grew wider, and she dropped her hand. "You look good for an old man."

Laughing, he returned to the seat. Dropped into it. The stitches in his side gave a minute tug on his flesh and he pressed his hand to them. Definitely needed to cut them out as soon as he could. "Thank you." He lifted the bottle, turning it again. "So I was there, and I was attacked, and lost a tooth during the fight. He hit me while I was human, but it tore from my jaw mid-shift. I guess that's why it was so different. Why it was not quite a dire wolf tooth and not quite a human tooth."

"Did you win?"

He snorted at the unexpected question. She never asked what he thought she would, never reacted the way he expected. He loved that.

Love?

Chest tightening, he stared at the bottle in his hand. "Let's just say if you ever met a one-armed, one-legged mountain lion shifter, it might be best not to mention you know me."

She raised her eyebrows and then pulled a serious face. "Oh, I'll be sure not to. Thanks for the warning."

A wave of warmth flowed through him and he smiled. How could he be enjoying this conversation? It was such a painful part of his past, the guilt of Basia, the brutal fight with the other shifter, almost dying himself... He shouldn't be enjoying himself.

But that's the thing, isn't it? Every minute you've ever spent with Amber, you've enjoyed. All those minutes in the café, when you thought she was just a vet, all the minutes spent with her as she struggled so hard to save you, care for you... Every minute is wonderful. She's wonderful. And you feel wonderful when you're with her. It's as simple as that.

Swallowing the thick lump in his throat, he met her gaze. "So, that's the story of the tooth."

It didn't matter how wonderful it all was, it was still dangerous. And he had to put a stop to it now.

CHEWING ON HER LIP, Amber digested what he'd told her. Or tried to. It was a lot to take in. She hadn't considered his age when she'd first discovered his existence. Hadn't considered there'd be others like him. A part of her must have assumed he wasn't the only one, but finding out he was sent a pang of sorrow through her. At least, the only dire wolf shifter, the last of his kind... A heavy lump settled in her stomach at the thought. To be alone, the only one, for centuries...

How had he stayed sane?

Or didn't it worry him? He'd done such an incredible job blending into society. Of existing in it.

And of trusting her with it all now.

Head buzzing, eyes prickling, she looked at him. "Okay," she finally said with a nod. "Thank you."

"You're welcome. Now, your turn." He leaned forward, resting his elbows on his knees. "Tell me about you. The real you."

Her cheeks grew warm and she tucked a non-existent strand of hair behind her ear. "You mean, the Amber who isn't a veterinarian from L.A.?"

A smirk tugged at the edges of his mouth. "Yes. Tell me about Amber the paleontologist who has two older brothers who seem very protective."

She snorted. "Well, Amber the paleologist lost her parents in a car accident when she was only little," she said.

The words felt rough in her mouth. Talking about her dead parents, the accident...it still affected her, even after all these years.

Closing her eyes, she drew a steadying breath, picturing them.

"They were Italian. Dad was a zoologist. Mom an English interpreter. She got a job working at the Italian embassy here in L.A. when Ray and Mick were five. They all moved here, Dad started working at the L.A. Zoo, and five years later, boom, I was born." Her grin stretched wide, and then faded. "I was almost ten when they died. I went to a boarding school and Ray and Mick looked after me, raised me, whenever school was out, until I was old enough to go to college."

"That must have been hard." Sorrow swam in Kitt's eyes. He shook his head, watching her.

She wobbled her head and shrugged. "They were amazing. And over protective. And scared off any boyfriend I tried to have. *That* was annoying."

He chuckled, even as the hand not holding the cola bottle clenched. "I bet," he said, voice low and almost a growl.

Jealous? Was he jealous?

A horde of butterflies took flight in her stomach and she hid her nervous sigh in a hitchy laugh. "Ray let me keep any stray I found—whether it was a dog or a cat or a lizard."

"Lizard?"

She smiled and ducked her head. "Hey, I was twelve at the time. When you're twelve and you find a lizard on the sidewalk that lets you pick it up without *too* much effort, you bring it home with you, okay?"

"Oh, of course you do." He dropped his own head, his laugh playing with her sanity. God, she loved the sound of it.

"Anyways," she went on, wriggling her butt a little on the mattress, "Ray let me keep any stray I found whenever I was home from boarding school, and made sure it had a good home to go to before I'd head back. And Mick taught me how to fight. And made sure my science grades were always the best they could be. And introduced me to all the best classic movies. It was Mick who got me interested in dinosaurs. He sat me down one summer break—I think I was thirteen—and made me watch all the Jurassic Park movies with him. By the time the first one finished, I was hooked. I became a fossil nerd. I made them take me to the La Brea Tar Pits that many times I think I could have got a job there as a guide. I think they were both happy when I went to college in San Francisco so they didn't have to look at a fossil again."

"I can't imagine anyone being happy you left their lives," Kitt said.

The low words, uttered with an almost casual calm, sent a shard of something warm and tight into her core.

She looked down at her fingers, playing with the hem of her cargo pants, and let out a choppy laugh. "Yeah, you're probably right. They're still over-protective and always sticking their noses into my life."

She thought of Ray. Knocked out on his clinic's floor. She hoped he was okay. She hoped he'd forgive her.

Lifting her head, she gave Kitt another shrug. "So I went to college, to study paleontology, and that's where I discovered dire wolves. And kinda got a bit hung up on them. Of course, I'd started reading George. R. R. Martin's *Song of Ice and Fire* series by then which probably didn't help."

Kitt let out an exasperated groan, and rolled his eyes with melodramatic weariness.

She grinned. "Oh shush. Do you have any idea how famous you'd be if the world knew about you? Everyone who reads that series, everyone who *watches* the TV show wants a dire wolf as a pet."

"I'm no one's pet," he growled, arching an eyebrow.

A charge energy radiated from him. He sat motionless, and yet she didn't doubt at any given second he could move. Fast. So fast she wouldn't know he had.

"Does that mean," she said, holding his stare, "you'll say no if I ask you to roll over so I can rub your belly?"

An iridescent golden light flickered in his eyes. His nostrils flared. "My wolf would probably love that."

"Your wolf?" A ribbon of excitement unfurled through her. An image of the massive dire wolf she'd watched sprinting through the forest in the Topanga Canyon hills filled her head. Her pulse quickened at the thought of combing her fingers through its thick fur.

His thick fur.

She caught her lip, and watched Kitt straighten from the chair.

Approaching her slowly, his lips curled. "*I* however..."

The ribbon of excitement twisted into a knot of anticipation. She gazed up at him as he drew to a halt directly in front of her. The pit of her stomach clenched. Her mouth grew dry. Her nipples beaded, turning into hard points in her bra.

"You wouldn't want your belly rubbed?" she whispered, brushing her hand against his bare stomach.

His sculpted abdominal muscles coiled beneath her palm. His swift intake of breath cut the room's silence.

She lowered her focus to where her hand touched his skin. Marveled at the sublime perfection of his abs.

Her blood roared in her eyes. Her heart hammered in her throat.

Swiping her tongue over her bottom lip, she inched her hand a little lower, skimming the shallow dip of his navel, before moving her fingers higher again.

A low groan vibrated through his body but he didn't move. Didn't stop her.

Licking her lips again, she lifted her head, her stomach clenching, her entire *core* clenching at the muted golden glow burning in his eyes.

At the unmistakable desire burning even hotter there.

"I want to kiss you, Kitt," she whispered. "I know what I did, the way I deceived you was unforgivable, but I really want to kiss—"

He lowered his head and brushed his lips over hers.

Gently at first, a choppy groan falling from him as she tentatively touched his tongue with hers.

Pressing his palm to her jaw, he deepened the kiss.

Took from her what she gladly and willingly offered. She slid her tongue over his again, shy and then not shy. Hungry.

A deep rumble vibrated in his chest and he moved his hand, gripping her braid for an intense second before cupping the back of her head.

She moaned, and mimicked his hold, every sense in her body thrumming at the cool strands of his hair against her fingers as she tugged him down to the bed with her. As she lifted one leg and slid her foot up and down the back of his thigh.

Tearing his lips from hers, he gazed down at her. "This can never work, Am," he whispered, pleasure warring with grief on his face. "You're human, and I'm not. My lifetime extends into centuries—on the assumption I'm not killed by a *Monstrum Venator*. Yours is constrained by human biology."

"I don't care," she whispered.

His nostrils flared. His hard length throbbed at the junction of her thighs. "Every second with me puts you in even greater danger."

She let out a breathy chuckle, and slid her foot up and down his thigh again. "Again, I don't care. Now will you shut up and just—"

He crushed her lips with his.

HE'D BEEN DRAWN to her from the second they first met, a meeting he now knew she'd staged to learn more about him, to study him. He'd been attracted to her from that very moment; emotionally, mentally, sexually.

And now, here they were, locked away in a motel room together, momentarily lost to the world.

Her kissed her, hungry and nervous and burning up with desire and need.

He'd never wanted to kiss someone like this before. Never wanted to share something of himself in the action.

And he shouldn't now. Everything he'd said was true.

But it didn't matter.

Not at that moment.

At that moment, the only thing that mattered was being with her.

Deep inside, the wolf he was growled. There was nothing angry or violent about the sound, the reaction. His inner animal joined in his pleasure, his joy.

Liquid heat pooled low in his groin. His body tingled, an ancient need to copulate surging through him. To flip her onto her stomach, mount her. Mate with her. Bite her on the back of her neck.

Mark her his property.

No.

Pulling away, he stared down at her, breath bursting from her.

"Am," he rasped. Hell, was that fear in her eyes? "I...I'm not...*human*, remember."

She lifted a shoulder, the dimple teasing her right cheek again. "Big deal."

"I've never done," he swallowed, "*this* with a human."

Her eyebrows dipped into a frown. "Are you...I mean, you'd stay in your human form while it's...y'know..." Her cheeks turned bright red and she caught her bottom lip with her teeth. "Wouldn't you?"

"What? Yes, hell yes." A wobbly laugh fell from him. "I'd never shift during...not with you." He dropped his face into his hand, and shook his head. "Christ, this is an awkward conversation."

Soft fingers touched his arm, lifting his head.

Amber kneeled in front of him, frown still firmly in place.

"I'm sorry," he muttered.

"I'll make you a deal," she said, corners of her lips twitching. "You stay human, and I won't write about *this*—" she waved her index finger back and forth between them, "—in my paper?"

He raised his eyebrows. "Your paper? You're still going to write that?"

She grinned, eyes twinkling with mischief. "How else am I going to become famous?"

Shaking his head again, he frowned at her. "I have no idea if you're serious or not, but I don't care. Not right now. All I want to do right now is..."

Fuck her. Mate with her. Claim her. Mark her.

"Kiss me stupid?" she suggested.

"Kiss you stupid," he confirmed, heart racing.

He would control his primal side. He'd constrain it.

And if you can't?

He could. For Amber, he could. He would.

"Then do it," she said, closing the small distance between them on the bed on her hands and knees. She stopped in front of him, holding his stare with hers as she brushed her lips against his. "Kiss me." A playful laugh left her. "Stupid."

He did. With a laugh, a growl and a groan, he snagged her braid again and crushed her mouth with his. Swiped his tongue into it, captured hers with hungry lashes.

She flattened her body to his, wrapped her arms around his neck, and rolled her hips, the soft curve of her sex rubbing against his thickening length.

Pleasure rushed through him. Hot and tight and absolute. His inner wolf barked and howled, charged and hyper aware, and then retreated, withdrawing from the moment.

Good. This was between Kitt and Amber; a man and a woman.

Groaning into her mouth, he smoothed his hands down her back and cupped her ass cheeks, hauling her closer still to his arousal.

She laughed—the sound dirty and playful—and nipped his bottom lip.

A ribbon of raw lust unfurled through him, sinking into his groin. His cock pulsed in his sweatpants, impatient and demanding.

"I felt that," Amber murmured, rolling her hips again.

"Did you now?" He kneaded her butt cheeks and pushed his groin forward. "It doesn't scare you? How much I want you?"

"It should, I guess." She looked up at him. "But no. I've...I've imagined stripping you naked and banging your brains out for a while now."

Throwing back his head, he laughed. "You are unlike any human I know, Dr. Calegari."

She beamed. "Thank you. Now, about that *kissing me stupid* thing..."

He crushed her lips with his again, one hand at the back of her head, the other sliding up over her hip, her waist, her ribcage.

Moaning, she closed her fingers around his wrist and placed his hand completely on her breast.

Hot pleasure rushed through him. Deep inside his existence, he lifted his head and howled again. He moved his lips over hers, making love to her mouth as he cupped and squeezed her breast. Her nipple rubbed at the center of his palm, an intoxicating friction that detonated fresh heat in his groin.

Dragging his lips from hers, he charted a path down her throat, gently tugging on her braid as he did so.

She rolled her head to the side, giving his mouth greater access to her smooth flesh.

"Oh wow..." she breathed, nails raking over his shoulders. "You really know how to..." He nipped her collarbone and she gasped, the sound dissolving into a laughing groan. "Oh wow," she said again.

He lifted his head, took her lips in his and, kissing her slowly, pressed her onto her back to lay between her thighs. Their groins nestled against each other, heat to heat, and a low, raw groan of approval vibrated through her body.

Arching her spine, she ground her sex to his and snagged his wrist again and moved his hand back to her breast. Under the soft cotton of her top.

His palm kissed the warm curve of her flesh and the soft lace of her bra.

Lace.

His head swum. Something about the fact she wore a lace bra on a dire-wolf hunting mission flooded his body with excitement and delight.

Her nipple beaded against his palm and he raised his head, another rush of liquid desire surging through him at the open pleasure on her face. "I want..." He swallowed. Tried again. "Am...I want to..."

The request stuck in his throat. It was too much. Too quickly. He'd scare her.

Lowering his head, he kissed her again. Worshipped her mouth with his tongue and teeth and lips.

She rolled her hips and raked her foot up and down

the back of his thigh, nails doing the same to his back and shoulders. Demanding more.

He journeyed his lips down over her throat once more, but this time, she fisted her hands in his hair and pulled his head up. "If you don't suck my nipple this time, Kitt, you're in big trouble."

Fuck, yes.

"Yes, doctor." Breath hot in his lungs, skin prickling with lust, he inched her top up, tugged aside the delicate lace cup covering her left breast, and took the dusky-pink puckered nub of her nipple in his mouth, sucking on it hard.

"Oh God, yeah," she groaned, one fist balling tighter in his hair, the other clawing at the back of his neck.

He lost himself to the exquisite sensation of her flesh against his tongue, between his teeth.

She arched beneath him again, her moans low and ragged. "I like that," she breathed.

Chuckling, he lifted his head. "I'm glad."

She grinned at him. "You're very good at—"

"*Rover!*" A male shout tore the air. "*Are you okay? Dak's worried sick.*"

Amber squealed and yanked down her shirt front. Kitt scrambled off the bed, scanning the room, growl tearing from his throat.

James Hastin stood in front of the TV, the motel's pay-per-view movie catalogue menu visible through his translucent form. The djinn looked at him, looked at Amber, and looked at him again. "Ah, shite. Sorry. Seems you are." He flicked Amber another look, and then dipped into a quick bow. "Go about your business. I'll tell Dak and Kade you're..." his lips twitched, "...fine and dandy."

With a click of his fingers, he disappeared.

"What. The hell..." Amber whispered, staring at the TV. "Did I... Was there..." She turned wide eyes to Kitt. "What just happened?"

Grinding his teeth, Kitt dragged a hand through his hair. Cock-blocked by the genie boy. Perhaps it was time to have a chat with the other Guarded Souls team members about personal space. Having each other's backs was incredible and wonderful and reassuring, but there had to be a line.

How many times has James saved one of the crew by projecting himself to their location, though?

Many times. But maybe the genie needed some kind of warning system before just appearing somewhere. Or better yet, there needed to be some kind of non-human equivalent of hanging a tie on the doorknob so he knew to keep his translucent ass away.

"Kitt?"

With another shaky sigh, he dropped onto the end of the bed. "That was James. He works with me at Guarded Souls."

"I could see through him," she pointed out, eyes growing wider. "And then he disappeared."

"Yeah, he does that sometimes. He's..." How did he say this? How would she react? "He's a djinn. A genie."

She blinked. "A what?"

He raked a hand through his hair. "A genie."

"A genie." She frowned. "But he's not blue."

Kitt snorted. If only James had stuck around to hear that. "He lost a bet with Dak once. Had to spend a week being blue, complete with a top-knot and earring."

She gaped at him. "What?"

He shook his head. "My work colleagues can be bastards sometimes."

Her eyebrows shot up.

"Right. Genie." Sighing, he shifted his butt on the bed and met her expectant stare. "Amber, there's a whole world of non-human beings living amongst mankind."

"*More* than just dire wolf shifters?"

God, she was taking this well. Would it be wrong to kiss her again?

Probably not so much wrong, but ill-conceived, given their current conversation.

"More than just my kind," he said, a heavy lump settling in his stomach. "As an aside, I'm the *last* of my kind."

Why did he tell her that? She didn't need to know that, and saying it aloud still tore at his soul.

Pain filled Amber's eyes and she reached her hand toward him before pulling it back. "I'm sorry. Kitt."

"It's okay." It had to be.

"So James is a genie," she said, voice husky. "Is Nathanial a genie as well?"

"Nath?"

"You mentioned him and James back at Ray's clinic."

"Ah. Nathanial's an angel."

Her eyebrows shot up again. "You're kidding?"

He shook his head. "No. Although I've never seen his wings. Christen has—he's a wight, by the way. A Norse nature spirit. I think they had a pissing contest about who's wings were bigger."

She blinked once more. "Now you're just making up shit to..." She stopped at his laugh. "Seriously?"

He nodded with a smile. "It's true. Promise."

"So an angel and a genie are protecting my brother?" She jumped her gaze all over the room, shaking her head. "Wow. I don't..." Lifting her hands to beside her head, she flung them to the side, fingers splaying. "Ka-boom."

He laughed again. "It's a little like that. My kind—non-humans, I mean—tend to keep it all on the downlow. Most of us are decent folks, just getting on with our lives, going about day to day routine the same way humans do. Guarded Souls is a legit security and personal protection agency with human clients and auxiliary staff, but the main protection team...we're an eclectic group of para-normal beings who deal with *other* paranormal beings who decide to not play nice with humanity."

"So you protect people no matter what the danger?"

He grinned. "At your service."

"Holy crap." She smiled back. "I knew you were incred-ible, but I didn't know just how much."

"Yeah yeah. Flattery will get you everywhere."

Her lips twitched. "Will it now?"

She crawled toward him on the bed.

Heart thumping fast, blood flowing south in a hurry, he narrowed his eyes at her. "You're taking this whole revela-tion well."

She wriggled her eyebrows. "I'm a paleontologist, remember. Discovering new things turns me on. Espe-cially new things about *old* things."

"Ah." He affected a wounded expression. "And here I was thinking it was just me and my duel existence that pressed your—" She silenced him with a kiss.

Grabbed two fistfuls of his hair, sought out his tongue with hers, and climbed onto his lap.

He groaned, letting the sound turn to a hungry growl as he grabbed her ass, kneading the curves of her cheeks with far from gentle fingers.

She moaned her approval and rolled her hips, rubbing the junction of her thighs against his engorged length.

His inner wolf stirred, and retreated again. Sated by Kitt's rising pleasure.

A euphoric wave rushed through him at the retreat of the animal side of his existence, just as raw desire for Amber—human desire, male desire—overwhelmed him.

Twisting around, he flattened her to her back on the bed, raking a hand down her side, over her hip and up the back of her thigh as she wrapped her leg around him.

The course fabric of her camouflage pants scratched against his palm and, with an impatient grunt, he broke away from the kiss. "I want you naked with me, Am."

"Never thought you'd ask," she panted, wriggling beneath him as she hooked her fingers around the bottom of her tank top.

Letting out a chuckle, he snagged the hemline, yanked it up over her head and tossed her shirt aside.

She laughed, wasting no time undoing her fly.

"Help me," she ordered, shimmying the waistband of her pants down over her hips.

"Gladly." He grabbed a fistful of the outside of each leg even as his stare fell on her breasts jiggling in her bra.

A rush of lust surged through him and, before he knew what he was doing, he pulled her pants off her legs with an impatient growl.

Not quite wolf, not quite human.

6

Amber gasped, lips parted, and closed her eyes. "Holy hell, that sound makes me horny."

Liquid heat sank into his groin. His heart hammered harder in his chest. Watching her face, he smoothed his hands down the inside of her legs, curled his fingers around her ankles and inched them apart. Enough to kneel between her calves. "It doesn't scare you?" he asked. "The growl?"

Opening her eyes, she smiled up at him. "Are you kidding? Would I be lying here like this with you if it did?"

Fresh pleasure rushed through him and, lowering his gaze, he devoured her almost naked body with his eyes.

Lacy black bra, and matching panties that sat low on the perfect curve of her hips, and...

"Is that a tattoo?" He leaned forward, tracing his fingertip over the small charcoal gray mark peaking above the lace band of her panties on her right hip.

Without waiting for an answer, he hooked his blunt fingernail against the lace and slowly pulled it down.

A small but exquisite tattoo of a howling dire wolf inked her skin, its lush fur ruffled by an invisible breeze.

"Told you I have a thing for *canis dirus*," she murmured.

He looked back up at her, breath shallow. The ink, its subject... His head roared. His body ached, wanting her on a level he'd never experienced before.

"It hurt like hell." She touched it with her fingertips. "But I've never regretted getting—"

Her husky words stopped as his lips touched the tattoo.

"Oh yeah..." she exhaled. "Definitely no regrets here."

He traced his tongue over the art and then, with reverent fingers, removed her panties completely, kissing her inner thighs, her calves, her ankles as he did so.

"I wonder if Alan Grant ever did this?"

He lifted his head at her wobbly whisper.

She stared at the ceiling, palm pressed to her forehead, a smile playing with her lips.

"I'd say yes," he said, drawing lazy patterns up her shins with his fingers. "From my experience, paleontologist are the most incredible sexual creatures in bed."

"Your experience?" The smile stretched into a grin as she looked at him.

He nodded. "My experience."

Eyebrows lifting, she rested her upper body on her elbows and studied him with mischievous eyes. "And that's vast and inexhaustible, is it?"

Dancing his fingers farther up her inner thighs, he grinned back. "Well, it's...this. Right now. Do I need any more evidence?"

She laughed. "Well, traditional scientific dogma would suggest you'd need more than just *one* experience to support your hypothesis but as far as *I'm* concerned *this* experience is more than—"

He parted her thighs with gentle hands and traced the tip of his tongue over their very junction.

"Ohhhhhkay..." she groaned, lifting her hips. "Experience away, baby."

He chuckled, moving his mouth up over her hip, across her hitching belly, and up one side of her body.

A hiccuppy giggle fell from her and she wriggled away. "That tickles."

Delight licked through him, and he nibbled at the sensitive curve of her waist again.

Another giggle. Another wriggle.

"Oh, I like this," he murmured, smiling down at her as he trailed his fingers over her other side. "Where else are you ticklish?"

He slid his lips up over her ribcage, and flicked her nipple with his tongue through the lace of her bra.

Her raw groan vibrated through her body into his, and he chuckled again. "So not ticklish there?"

With a throaty laugh, she fisted a hand in his hair and made him look at her. "I should warn you," she said, the words as husky as her laugh, "I'm a tickling master. So unless you want to spend the next hour at my mercy..."

"Sounds perfect."

She rolled her eyes, lips twitching as she mock glared at him. "Unless you want to spend the next hour at my tickling mercy, I'd suggest you get back to the matter at hand."

He arched an eyebrow. "Would you now?" he said, inching his palm down over her belly. "*This* matter at hand?" He stroked his finger over her warm folds.

Closing her eyes, she let out a happy sigh. "Yes. That. That matter at— Oh God, yes!" she cried, as he sort out her very center with a smooth thrust of his finger.

He lost himself in her body, in her response to his touch. Long minutes spent tasting her, learning every crevice and curve of her body.

His own body reacted to every sound she made. When they both battled with her bra to undo its clasp, her exasperated laugh almost drove him over the edge. How could a simple sound turn him on so much?

"Kitt..." she whispered, combing her fingers through his hair as he worshipped first her right breast, and then her left. They were perfect. They filled his hand as if made for them. "Kitt..."

Releasing her nipple with a pop, he met her gaze. "Yes?"

She smiled. "Get your pants off."

He laughed, climbed off the bed and stripped his sweatpants from his body.

"Holy crap," she whispered.

Hot pleasure lashed through him at her words. He stood motionless, letting her run her gaze over his naked form.

"You are the most...well-endowed *canis dirus* I've ever encountered," she said, flicking him a grin.

A spasm claimed his erect cock at her compliment.

She let out a long sigh, and made her way to the edge of the bed on her knees. "Can I..." She held out her hand.

Heart thumping, breath tight, he stepped back to her.

She closed her fingers around him. Squeezed him.

And lowered her head...

A growl tore from him, low and carnal and not at all human. His skin prickled. Every fiber of his being grew hot.

With every swipe of her tongue on his flesh, with every nip of her teeth, he became more lost to her.

When she lifted her head, replacing her mouth with a firm hand, he sucked in a steadying breath.

Control. Control it...

"We don't have a condom," she murmured.

Shit. They didn't.

He carried one in his wallet, but his wallet was—he hoped—still in his jeans pocket, back in the Guarded Souls safe house up in the Topanga Canyon hills. Had any of the team been there since James's situation? And if so, had they collected up his clothes where he'd left them on the floor before running from the safe house naked, shifting into his dire wolf form a few feet from the door?

Does it matter now?

No. What matter was he wanted to make love to the most incredible woman he'd ever known, and she was human and he didn't have a fucking condom.

Clenching his jaw, he clawed a hand through his hair. "I'll go get one."

She looked up at him. "I don't..." A faint pink heat painted her cheeks. "I mean...if it means anything, I have an IUD, and as ridiculous as it probably sounds, I trust you more than I trust any—"

He crushed her mouth with his, pressing her flat to the bed.

Covering her body with his.

His erection nudged her damp folds. Parted them.

Heat roared through him. She moaned into his kiss, wrapping her legs around his hips. Locking her ankles at the small of his back.

Deep inside, his wolf stirred. Ready.

Control. Control...

Lifting his head, he cupped her face in his hands and held her gaze with his. "I'll try to be gentle."

She shook her head, lips curling. Pleasure burned in her eyes. Her heart pounded against his chest. Fed his own lust and need. "Don't you freaking dare."

A shaky laugh fell from him. "In that case..."

He captured her lips again, unleashing his hunger for her as he sank deep into her.

"Oh my God," she cried out, arching into his thrust. "Yes!"

They moved together. In perfect rhythm.

Moved as one, their breaths mingling, their fingers threading together.

She moaned his name, and squeezed her legs tighter around him.

He growled into the side of her throat, his thrusts growing faster, wilder.

His body burned, his skin prickled, and when he feared he'd lost control of his duel existence, when the concentrated pleasure of being inside her pushed him beyond what he'd ever experienced before, he threw back his head and howled.

And at the primitive sound, Amber slammed her hips upward, took all of his length deeper still, and cried out his name, her inner muscles pulsing around him, her release propelling him to his.

He emptied himself into her, human body on fire, mind blurring between human and animal, and then, with another howl inside his duel existence, his wolf faded back to its waiting place. Sated.

Slowing his thrusts until he grew still between her legs, he lowered his gaze to hers. A wobbly laugh fell from him and he pressed his forehead to her chest. "That...wasn't as long as I wanted."

Sliding her legs from around his hips, she snared a

fistful of his hair and lifted his head. "That was incredible."

Without withdrawing from her—no way he was ready to do that—he kissed her. Slowly. Explored her lips with his.

Showed her how incredible she was with his mouth.

And as he kissed her, as he lost himself to her sounds and taste and touch again, his body responded, and they were moving as one again, and nothing else was important except being with her.

THEY ORDERED PIZZA AN HOUR LATER. Or maybe it was two. He truly had no idea what time it was, and Amber didn't seem to care either.

Pepperoni, olives and pineapple. Who knew he'd finally find someone who also liked pineapple on their pizza. No one at Guarded Souls did and gave him grief any time he tried to order it.

The pizza arrived a few minutes later, while she was in the shower.

She wandered out of the bathroom naked, her skin still damp, the delicate scent of soap filling his breath, a heartbeat after Kitt closed the door, pizza box in hand.

"Is it really pizza you want to eat?" she asked, leaning her back against the bathroom doorframe and sliding her hands up above her head, a devilish light in her eyes.

He tossed the box on the bed and lunged at her.

Half an hour later, maybe more, they devoured the pie cold, scrolling through the TV channels.

"I paid for a movie I didn't watch," she grumbled, cross-legged on the bed beside him, pouting at the TV. She'd dressed once again in her camo cargo pants and black tank top, although he had no idea where her bra was. "Us paleontologists aren't made of money." She arched a sideways look at him. "Rescuing dire wolf shifters is turning out to be expensive stuff."

"Do you regret it?" He adjusted his head in his hand and stretched out a little more on his side.

She rolled her eyes. "No. In fact..."

Tossing the TV remote aside, she pressed a hand to his chest and flattened him to his back, straddling his hips.

He laughed, closing his hands around her hips as she bent at the waist and kissed him. "You taste like pepperoni," she whispered against his lips.

"You like pepperoni?" he whispered back, inching his palms up her ribcage.

"I'm Italian remember," she murmured, rolling her hips to stroke the junction of her thighs to his thickening length. "Well, my parents were. Pepperoni's in my blood."

He chuckled again, nipped her lips and smoothed his hands up to cup one of her full breasts as he kissed her again.

Pleasure and joy and something far more significant and unnerving flowed through him. He could do this forever. Wanted to do it forever.

Would it be wrong to just shut out the rest of the world and spend the rest of their lives doing this? Discovering each other's bodies and desires?

The dinosaur fossils weren't going anywhere, and Guarded Souls could do without one team member for... well, ever. Kade would understand. So would the rest of the team.

Lifting his head from hers, he feathered the backs of his fingers over her cheek. "I know this isn't what you'd planned when you *accidently* bumped into me at the coffee house..." She dropped her gaze, cheeks growing pink. "But I'm glad you did. Not because you saved me from the hunter, but because..."

He trailed off. Grew still.

Every hair on his body stood on end.

His skin prickled. His muscles coiled.

Stare sliding to the door, he drew a slow breath. Tasted the air.

Someone stood the outside their room. Silent. Motionless.

Someone whose scent was tainted by the stench of the warehouse.

Someone who'd *been* in the warehouse.

Deep within him, his wolf snarled. Crouched.

"Kitt?' Amber whispered, pressing closer to him. Her heart pounded in her chest, thumping through him. "What's going on?"

He narrowed his eyes, stare locked on the door.

And moved as the soft electronic buzz of the lock releasing shattered the silence of the room and the door-knob turned.

IN A BLUR.

Everything moved in a blur.

The room as Kitt shoved her backward to the mattress. Kitt as he lunged for the opening door.

Except it wasn't Kitt anymore, but a massive grey dire wolf wearing sweatpants.

Lunging at the man charging into the room, gun draw.

Lunging at—

"Mick!" she screamed, throwing herself off the bed.

Her brother swung toward her and everything stopped being a blur and became slow motion.

Hideous, vivid slow motion.

The dire wolf—Kitt—destroyed the small distance between him and Mick, hackles raised, terrifying fangs barred. Mick reeled backward, gun locked on Kitt, eyes wide.

"*No!*" Amber screamed, just as Kitt's massive front paws slammed into Mick's chest. "*Kitt, stop!*"

Mick smashed into the floor. The solid thud of his skull smacking the hard surface proceeded the clank of his gun falling from his grip by a split second.

The growl of the dire wolf tore apart the air and Amber threw herself forward, just as the wolf drove its open muzzle at Mick's throat.

And then everything got fast again.

Real fast.

Her shoulder hit the dire wolf first, driving into its solid side. Pain shot through her—the kind that came from ramming your shoulder into a mountainside—and then she tumbled forward, crashing into the floor as the wolf twisted toward her.

"*Kitt,*" she cried, flinging her hands up, protecting her face.

Fangs barred, the dire wolf grew still. Stared at her, eyes glowing golden light, growl rumbling deep in its chest.

"Amber," Mick snarled, "move."

She heard his gun click. The dire wolf's ears twitched.

And then she scrambled forward, throwing herself once again at the wolf. Throwing herself between Kitt and her brother. "Mick, stop!"

"*Get out of the way, sis,*" Mick scream, gun pointed at her, at Kitt. "*Get out of the*—"

The air shifted behind her, as if sucked in and blasted out, and Kitt—*human* Kitt—grabbed her, yanked her behind his body, and charged at Mick.

Amber's hip collided with the room's small table. She bounced off it, stars exploding in her eyes, just as Kitt's fist collided with Mick's jaw.

She cried out, in pain, in fear, in confusion, and staggered forward, reaching for Kitt. She had to stop him. She had to stop him killing her brother...

"Kitt!" She grabbed at his arm, its sweat-slicked surface slipping under her fingers as he punched his fist toward Mick's face again. "Stop it! It's my brother."

Kitt froze. Dropped his arm, and looked at her over his shoulder, eyes still glowing. "Brother?" he asked, voice an animalistic growl.

"Br—"

Mick slammed his joined fists into the side of Kitt's neck.

"Mick!" she screamed, just as Kitt—with another terrifying growl—snapped back to Mick and smashed his fist into Mick's jaw.

Down.

Mick went down.

With a solid, heavy thud.

"What the fuck?" She shoved Kitt out of the way and fell to her knees beside Mick. He groaned, eyes rolling, and then slumped motionless. "Mick?"

Snapping her glare up to Kitt—standing beside her, chest heaving, nostrils flaring—she shook her head. "Why do you keep punching out my brothers?"

"Why is Ray here?" he growled, eyes bright and far

from human. "He should be under Guarded Souls protection. He smells like the warehouse which means—"

"This is *Mick*." She threw up her hands. "They're identical twins. You just punched out Mick, the forensic detective. The one who called me from the freaking warehouse."

Kitt's nostrils flared again.

"He saw the cage and blood and the footprints, remember? He's not a bad guy."

She turned back to Mick, splayed on the floor, eyes shut, out cold.

Oh boy. He was never going to warm to Kitt now.

Warm to?

A laugh burst from her. Yeah, like there was *any* chance Mick was going to play nice older-brother to the guy who turned into a massive dire wolf in front of his eyes. Kitt knocking him out wouldn't even be a factor in the not-with-my-sister-you're-not routine Mick would fire at Kitt.

"Oh God," she groaned through a laugh. "I don't even know what do to now."

Behind her, Kitt drew a slow, shaky breath. "Amber, I'm sorry. I just..."

"Acted on instinct?" She looked up at him, her stomach twisting. "I guess that's...sweet?

An unreadable expression flared in his eyes—once again human—and he looked away. "It's not. Nor is it forgivable."

She frowned up at him. Ached for the guilt and haunted grief in his face. "You're one-hundred percent healed now?" she asked, stomach knotting tighter. "Is that right? Is that why you changed your...shape?"

Pulling in another deep breath, he raked his hands through his hair. "I think so. When I woke up earlier, I could feel the ability to shift had returned. Whatever had been in the shit the hunter shot into me, it had left my system. Things were back to normal."

She nodded.

"Well, not normal," he said, gaze finding hers again. "I woke up next to you. That's not normal."

A heavy band wrapped around her chest. "I guess not."

And here she'd been, fantasizing about spending the rest of her life waking up to Kitt in her bed. His bed. Any bed.

Letting out her own choppy breath, she turned back to Mick. Yep, still out of it. "Y'know, you'd make a killing as a pro-boxer," she muttered, touching her fingers to the ugly bruise blooming over Mick's jaw.

"Can I have your phone, Amber?"

She twisted around to frown up at Kitt. "My... Why?"

He held out his hand, expression indecipherable. "Please?"

Pulling it out of the side pouch of her cargo pants, she gave it to him. Watched him tap something on its screen. "Who are you—"

"Hey, Kade," he said, gaze locked on Mick. "It's me. I need help. Can anyone get to my location right now?" He waited a second, eyes closing. "Okay. That'll do. Thanks."

Ending the call, he held out her phone, looking at it, not her.

"I can't take off and leave another brother, Kitt," she grumbled, taking her phone and tossing it onto the bed. Although of the twins, Mick was definitely the one most likely to be able to handle himself when he came to, or cause a problem, and she seriously wasn't ready for the ensuing conversation about dire wolf shifters. Not at all.

With a wry chuckle, he opened his eyes. "You're not, Am."

She let out a grunt. "Then you better be ready for a pissed-off forensic cop when he..." Trailing off, she narrowed her eyes. "Wait. You're leaving me here."

A cold fist squeezed her heart.

"No no." She shook her head. "Not after everything that's happened. I'm not letting you out of my sight."

"No one's going to believe your paper, Dr. Calegari," he murmured, dragging a hand through his hair, his eyes jumping around the room.

"Screw my paper." She jolted to her feet. "You think I'm going to let you go out there when this *Monstrum Venator* is still after you?"

He lifted an eyebrow. "I've survived over four-hundred years without you looking after me, Amber."

"And you'd probably be dead and stuffed by now if I hadn't hit the old bastard on the back of the head with a wrench." What was he thinking? Taking off? Without her? After everything they'd been through to—

Her stomach dropped. Her breath caught in her throat. "Oh God, are you taking off because we..."

He closed the distance between them in a single stride, cupped her face in his hands and kissed her.

"Yes," he murmured. "But not in the way you think." Stroking his thumb over her lips, he nudged her forehead with his. "The thought of you in danger tears me apart."

"I thought I was an easier target for the hunter if I wasn't with you." He was not doing this to her. No way.

He shook his head. "It's not the *Monstrum Venator* I'm worried about."

She pulled away a little. "I'm not scared of you, Kitt."

A ragged sigh tore from him and he stepped backward.

"That's the problem. You should be. What you've been through, what you saw just now, what I am. What I've done to your brothers...you should be more than scared."

The cold fist squeezed her heart again. "You don't get to tell me how to feel, Kitt."

Another wry chuckle fell from him and he took another step backward. "I would have loved spending the rest of my life arguing with you about this, Am. And all sorts of other things. You have no idea. You've got under my skin so much it's hard to think rationally. But I have to go. I have to."

She shook her head. "No. Just try and leave without me. I dare you. Just—"

He turned and—in a blur of inhuman speed—left the room.

So fast she couldn't tell if he was human or wolf.

She ran after him, stopping at the door when Mick groaned behind her. Heart thumping, she scanned the area beyond the motel, searching.

Looking. Praying...

Nothing. Just the parking area, and beyond that, the street and its busy traffic.

No sign of a half-naked man running barefoot away from the motel. No sign of a wolf larger than any living wolf had a right to be.

No sign of Kitt.

"Bastard," she muttered, slumping against the door-frame. She was going to make him pay for this when she saw him—

A blood-red motorbike pulled into the parking space beside her Prius, its rangy rider dressed in faded denim jeans, a black AC/DC T-shirt and beaten-up black leather biker boots.

Growing still, muscles coiling, she watched him kill the engine and remove a helmet just as battered as his boots.

"Amber Calegari?" he said plonking the helmet down on the gas tank and resting his elbows on it, the slightest hint of Australia accents dancing on the vowels of her name. "I'm Daku. Kade from Guarded Souls sent me."

7

C lothes.

He could run around LA all he liked looking for the hunter, but doing so in nothing but a pair of sweatpants wasn't smart.

A six foot six, bare-chested, bare-footed man who looked like he could rip a tree apart, running, sniffing, eyes glowing an unnatural golden hue would definitely draw too much attention.

You need sunglasses, a T-shirt at least, and a pair of runners for your feet.

Slowing to a jog through the Walmart entry, he pinpointed the menswear section and sped up.

He could go home, get what he needed there, but he didn't want to waste time. As it was, he'd already spent twenty-minutes running to the superstore.

He could also call in help from any of the team not currently on a job, but given he'd already tapped Nathanial to protect Ray, and now Dak to guard Amber, he couldn't bring himself to ask Kade for more.

Besides, what he'd said to the vampire hours ago—back in Ray's clinic—was true: this *was* personal.

The *Monstum Venator* had pissed him off, threatened Amber's life, all for a kill, a trophy and bragging rights.

Kitt was going to make him regret that.

When he found him.

So he needed to move around without drawing attention.

Which called for a little five-finger discounting. After he'd taken care of the hunter he'd come back and pay for what he was now taking. Pressing the sole of one half of a pair of generic running shoes to the bottom of his right foot, he scowled. Would these fit?

They'd have to. The store's security guard was watching him.

"Ha," he grunted, snagging a T-shirt from the rack as he headed for the exit. "If only you knew, buddy."

Now all he needed was a pair of sunglasses, dark ones, and he'd be good to go.

"Hey."

He jumped at the familiar female voice behind him. Snapped around, fists bunched.

"I could pay for those if you want?" the petite woman with the purple buzzcut said, pointing at the items in his hand, a smirk twisting her black-glossed lips. She flicked a devilish look over his shoulder. "Or do you want to be chased by the store's security?"

Without turning, Kitt sensed the large man approaching a few feet behind him.

"What are you doing here, Nim?" he asked, grimacing. "How'd you find me?"

Nim, Guarded Souls' resident wiccan shrugged. "I know a spell for how to find people. I also know you told

Kade hunting this *Monstrus Venabor* is personal, but I wanted to see if I could help."

"*Monstrum Venator.*"

She shrugged again. "Same same."

Letting out a ragged breath, he shook his head and began walking. "It's okay. I've got this."

Falling in beside him, she tugged the shoes and shirt from his hand. "Sure you do. That's why you just left Dak guarding the woman you've been pining over for a month and a half in a Holiday Inn. And her brother...is that right? Her brother? One of her brothers? Something like that. That's why one of her brothers is currently being shadowed by Nathanial. By the way, the angel says he will kick your ass if you don't let me help."

Kitt snorted. "Nathanial's a fine one to talk, given what happened to him just recently."

Nim laughed. "I know, right? What is it with you male paranormal beasties? Is it a testosterone thing? Is paranormal testosterone more annoying than the human kind?"

"You said you were here to help me, right?" He gave her another sideways glance. "Or did you say to insult me?"

She grinned. "Take your pick. Now tell me, apart from paying for your new wardrobe, thereby saving you from getting arrested for shoplifting, how can I help? Want me to cast a spell on the *Monster Venusaur*?"

"You're doing that on purpose now."

"Of course I am."

Sighing, he shook his head again. "The bastard is using magic. I don't want anyone else at risk."

"All the more reason for me to help out?"

"Don't you already have a client to be guarding?"

"The Instagram model? Her crazy fan got arrested at

two A.M. See? If you were at the staff meeting this morning instead of getting caught by a *Monstrum Venator* —" She grinned up at him, tapping the side of her nose "—you'd know these things."

"I see Kade's filled everyone in on my misadventures. Awesome." He dragged a hand down his face. "I'm never going to live this down."

"True. Getting caught by a monster hunter's pretty embarrassing, Kitt."

Shooting her a quick glance, he let a low growl rumble in his chest. "Says the wiccan who lost a witch fancy-dress competition last Halloween. I wonder where the nearest bucket of water is?"

Slapping her hand to her chest, she threw back her head in a silent, melodramatic laugh and then glared at him. "It's a good thing I like you."

He sighed again. "I like you too." It was impossible not to like Nim. "And thank you for the offer to help, but—"

She stopped, grabbing at his forearm. "Wait. Do you actually know where the hunter is now? I'm assuming you don't otherwise you'd be either on him already, or heading his way, rather than trying to get clothes to blend into society while you look for him." Her eyes twinkled, her latent magic swirling in their depths. "Want me to locate him for you? At least let me do that? It should be easy." She chewed her lip, and frowned. "Ish."

Kitt narrowed his eyes, his gut clenching.

Locating the *Monstrum Venator* in human form would take time. In a city the size of L.A. locating him in dire wolf form would *also* take time. And the longer he took, the more at risk Amber was. Dak couldn't watch her forever, and knowing her, she was unlikely making it easy for him to do so.

Unless he was prepared to sit and watch a movie with her, and as far as Kitt knew, Dak didn't even own a TV.

"How soon could you do it?" he asked, walking again. "I take it you'd do the same spell you used to locate me?"

"Depends. I always have on hand the things I need to locate the Guarded Souls team."

He raised an eyebrow. That little nugget of information would require a conversation. On another day.

She pulled a contemplative face. "To find the hunter... I'd need something personal of his. Any chance you've got something he owns? Or even better, is there any way we can get our hands on something that has his blood on it?"

Blood.

Drawing to a halt, he sucked in a swift breath, the image of the warehouse filling his head.

"What about a wrench covered in blood?" he asked.

Would the wrench Amber hit the hunter with still be in the warehouse? It was a crime scene after all. Did the cops clean up a crime scene immediately after? Take evidence—possibly weapons used—away for analysis?

Call Amber. Ask her to ask her brother...the forensic detective. Mick.

A dry snort tore at the back of his throat. What were the chances Mick would help? Given Kitt had not only put his little sister at risk, but knocked him out? Not to mention Mick had seen him shift into dire wolf form.

And caught you in bed with Am.

Yeah, Mick wouldn't help at all.

"I might be able to get my hands on something with the hunter's blood on it," he said. "But getting it might require a little bit of stepping outside what would normally be considered legal."

Nim's black-glossed lips stretched into a wide grin. "I'm in. What do we have to do?"

"Brother?"

Amber looked up from Mick's still face, frowning at the man leaning against the motel room's closed door. "Yes."

"Twin? Of the one Nathanial is guarding?"

"Yes."

Her heart thumped in her chest. The lump in her throat seemed to grow thicker. There was a still menace about Daku. A bottomless calm that stirred a disquiet in her. She wasn't scared by him, just uneased.

"What kind of non-human being are you?" she asked.

He studied her, dark eyes somehow absorbing the light. "The kind you don't want to know about."

She frowned again. "And you and Kitt are friends?"

He dipped his head in a single nod, turning his attention to TV.

A re-run episode of M*A*S*H played on the screen, the volume low enough the actors looked like they were all taking part in a silent movie.

"I like this show," Daku said. "Catchy theme song."

Amber frowned, and turned her attention back to Mick. Still unconscious. He was going to be insanely angry when he came to.

She'd called an ambulance the second Daku had closed the door, cheeks burning as she fumbled through the explanation on how Mick had been knocked out.

"Some guy," she'd mumbled at the dispatch's question. "I don't know him. He just punch my brother and ran away."

The lie would never stand up in court, but hopefully she'd be able to calm Mick down, explain everything as soon as he was conscious again.

He'd seen Kitt change after all.

On the floor, Mick groaned, eyelids flicking, creasing, and finally opening.

"Mick," she breathed, relieved.

His eyes rolled about for a split second before focusing on her. "Sis..." he slurred. And then his eyes snapped wide open and he scrambled to his feet, stare whipping around the place. "Where is he? Where's..."

"Mick!" she leaped to her own feet, grabbing at his arm. "Stop stop stop."

Daku levered himself off the door. Nothing about him conveyed anything apart from indifferent ease. "Think you need to sit down, mate."

Mick glared at him, fists balling. "Who the fuck are you?"

The smallest of smiles pulled at Daku's lips as he slid Amber a glance. "The being keeping you safe."

Mick snarled, swinging his gaze around the room. "Where's my gun?" He saw it on the bench where she'd placed it while he was unconscious and snatched it up. "Where's the fucker who...who..." He trailed off, turning back to Amber. "Did he...did I see him..."

From the corner of her eye, Amber saw Daku step toward them.

"Mick, you need to sit down," she damn near shouted, grabbing Mick's shoulders and forcing him to drop onto the end of the bed.

Huh, you and Kitt were making out on that very spot only a little while a—

"The chair," she blurted, pulling Mick off the bed and directing him to the chair. "Sit here. Better for your head."

Mick stared at her, stunned. "What on earth is going on, sis?"

She flicked Daku a look. Would he do something to Mick if her brother blurted out he'd seen Kitt shift form? Could he? Mick had a gun. And bulk. And a shit load of anger. She didn't know what kind of non-human Daku was, just that Kitt trusted him to protect her, but would he resort to violence to protect Kitt's secret?

Daku's dark eyes seemed to glint, and he gave his head a tiny shake.

Relief rushed through her. "It's okay," she said, to Mick, to Daku, to herself. "It's all going to be okay. The ambulance is coming." She gripped Mick's wrists tighter. "You had a bit of a...fall."

God, maybe getting the story straight from the start would have been wise.

"Don't *fall* me." Shaking off her hold, Mick straightened from the chair and turned to Daku. "I want answers. Who are you? Where's the guy who abducted Amber from Ray's clinic? The guy that knocked *him* out as well?"

Daku's eyebrows raised a fraction. "Who?"

Mick threw up his hands, swung his stare around the room again, and glared back at Amber. "Where is he?"

"Not here," she sighed. Swallowing, she looked up at her brother. "He's gone. So you don't have to worry about him anymore."

"Worry about him?" Mick gaped at her like she'd sprouted a second head. "I'm going to arrest the fucker. Or...or...get him thrown into some kind of...of...science lab. The guy changed..." He stopped, rubbing at his jaw as he turned to look at Daku.

Daku flashed a smile at him, and settled back against the door, ankles crossed, arms folded.

With a snarl, Mick turned back to Amber. "If we don't need to worry, why's *he* here? What have you got yourself into, sis? Is this all to do with that DNA test?"

"Umm..."

"I thought you were trying to work out if you were adopted, or something."

She blinked. "What?"

Mick dragged a hand through his hair, gaze skittering over the floor. "I know you always think you're so different to me and Ray, and I know you never really got to know Mom and Dad before they died. I thought..." He broke off, looking back at her, eyes shining, anguish etching his face. "I thought you didn't think you were really our sister."

"Oh my God, Mick." She threw herself at him. Wrapped her arms around his broad torso and hugged him. "Don't you ever think that."

His large arms smoothed around her back and he squeezed her. Tight. "I love you, sis." His voice cracked. "I've been scared out of my fucking mind these last twenty-four hours."

Pulling away a fraction, she smiled up at him. "I'm okay. Seriously. I'm okay."

He studied her eyes, searching for something, and then let out a wobbly breath. "Then why are you under some kind of guard from the wonder from Down Under over there?"

Daku snorted.

Amber gave him a warning scowl and then smiled up at Mick. Being hugged by her big brothers—either twin—was one of her favorite things in the world. They'd raised her, cared for her, loved her. As soon as all this settled down, as soon as she and Kitt worked out whatever she and Kitt had to work out—because be damned if she was letting him just run out of her life like that—she'd bring Ray and Mick up to speed.

They needed to know.

Whether they chose to believe her or not was a different matter, but she couldn't lie to them.

It tore her apart doing so.

"Daku—" she began.

"Happy for you to call me Dak," Daku said from the door.

She threw him a gentle scowl and looked back at Mick. "*Dak* is...making sure we're okay while someone dangerous is stopped."

"Stopped?" Mick grew still in her arms. "Someone dangerous is stopped. What the hell does that mean?"

"Can I explain later?"

He shot up his eyebrows. "Sure. How 'bout the next time Ray beats me at golf."

She groaned, letting him go to throw up her hands. Ray sucked at golf. "Mick, I just need you to trust me. Please? Dak is not going to let anything happen, and after I've spoken to Kitt...well, it'll be okay."

Mick's jaw bunched. "I don't like this Kitt guy, sis."

Her stomach knotted. "You don't have to like him. I do."

"And it means jack shit that he's beaten the shit out of both your brothers?" His expression grew dark. "Oh yeah, we're really going to approve of this one. Let's ignore the fact the guy seems to change into some great big fucking wolf when he's angry."

"He does *what*?" *No no, not ready for this. Not ready.* "I don't know what you think you saw but I can assure you..." She trailed off, blew at the wisps of hair hanging over her eyes, and threw up her hands again. "You know what, Mick. No. I'm not doing this. It's my life. Mine. Not yours, not Ray's. Mine. And I'll date whoever I want."

"Date?" His nostrils flared. "Not on my watch, kid."

"Screw you." She shoved at his chest, staggering back a step when he didn't move. "I'm not a kid. I'm thirty-four. I have a freaking doctorate, you asshole. If I want to date a dire wolf freaking shifter I can."

She froze. Swallowed.

Oh God, did she just say that?

From the door, Daku let out a low breath.

Mick grew motionless, jaw knotting. His stare held hers and slowly, slowly, he reached out and curled his finger around her right wrist. "That's enough, Amber."

She yanked her wrist free. Tried to. He clamped his fist tighter around it.

"Let me go, Mick." She glared at him. "You're being a dick."

"And you're being a slut."

"Hey." Daku's voice cracked on the air, like a thunder-clap in a storm.

Mick flinched, and then spun to face him, gun leveled straight at his chest. "This is none of your business."

"Mick, stop it," Amber snapped.

Daku crossed his ankles again, back to the door and met Mick's stare. "Mate, I've been inside Newton's dreams. I know exactly what he feels for your sister. And I *also* know he'd never talk to her like that. Or let anyone else do so, whether they were her brother or not."

Amber's breath burst from her. What? Daku had been *where*?

Aim unwavering, Mick narrowed his eyes. "You've been

inside his dreams..." He stopped, jaw clenching, studying Daku.

"Put the gun down, Mick," she said, touching his shoulder with tentative fingers. "You've had a shock. Some weird shit's happened. But you need to listen to me, and put the gun—"

A faint knock came at the door.

Two quick raps. Followed by two slow ones.

Daku stiffened, shoulders hunching and snapped his stare to Amber. "Amber," he growled. "Get—"

The door blew inward in a blast of black heat, and the last thing Amber saw was Daku flinging through the midnight-cloud, and the last thing she felt was Mick's arms wrapping around her, shielding her from the blast.

And then, nothing.

NIM FROZE, eyes growing wide, distant. Stunned. "Kitt!"

He stopped, the strip of police tape crisscrossing the warehouse door crunching in his hand. "What is it?"

"Magic," she whispered. "Dark magic. Someone's just attacked Daku with dark magic."

NOTHING.

Nothing...

And then...something...

...*THE CAGE RATTLED, the massive wolf inside barring its teeth at her. No, not at her. At...*

...is she dead? a tall shadow muttered.

The wolf snarled, hackles rising.

She twisted around, to see what it growled at.

The tall shadow stepped back into the darkness.

She better not be...

The wolf snarled again.

It's okay, Kitt, *she murmured, watching it.* We're okay. We're going to be okay.

The wolf paced the cage, and then sat, powerful haunches coiled.

Amber, *a calm voice said behind her.* Amber, I need you to open you eyes. I need you to see where you are.

She turned away from the wolf, to the voice, and smiled at the man with the dark hair and dark eyes standing behind her.

What are you doing here, Dak? *She frowned.* Why is it so...

If she's dead...*the shadow whispered,* you're time is...

Amber, *Dak said, as Kitt growled and snarled in the cage.* You need to open your eyes. I can't do anything until you open your eyes. Open your eyes and look where—

She's not dead. *Wrinkled hands shook her shoulder.* She's not...

A FAINT LIGHT prickled Amber's closed eyelids and she moaned, trying to open her eyes. Trying to drag herself out of the nothing. Out of the darkness.

Freezing air slid around her ankles, over her arms, her shoulders. Her entire body ached. Her head throbbed.

Open your eyes, a memory ordered in her head. *Open your...*

Amber opened her eyes, a scratchy groan falling from her.

Where was she?

Squinting, blinking against the dim light filtering in through a high unseen window, she took in her surroundings.

Not the warehouse she'd found Kitt. But like the warehouse.

Large and empty and musty. And cold.

She shifted, a part of her brain telling her she was tied to a plastic chair. "Hello?"

Her voice bounced around the emptiness, wafting back to her, tiny and weak.

She wriggled in the chair. Whatever bound her wrists cut into them, a scratching run.

Rope?

Seriously? Someone had tied her hands behind her back on a freaking chair?

Great.

"Mick?" she called.

His named floated back to her, weaker than her shouted hello.

"Daku?" she tried.

"Daku?" a male voice said from the darkness to her right.

His voice. Manson's. The hunter.

She snapped her head around, but all she could see was darkness.

Her flesh crawled. She didn't need to see Manson to know the hunter lurked in the shadows, watching her. She remembered his voice. Too easily.

"Why aren't you dead?" she snarled, fighting with the rope on her wrists. "Where's Mick? Where's Daku?"

"Mick doesn't interest me," the hunter said, unseen.

"But this Daku. Tell me about him. Am I right in believing he is a dreamwalker?"

"Bite me," she spat. Where was he? If she could see him...

What? If you could see him, what?

"I've never hunted a dreamwalker," Manson went on, voice now floating to her from behind. Bastard. Freaking bastard. "There aren't many of them. At least none worthy of my time."

A soft finger traced over the back of her neck and she screamed, jerking in the chair.

The ropes cut into her wrists again, and she grew still, staring at the floor and pulling in a steady breath.

Calm. Stay calm, Mick's voice reminded her.

Calm. Yeah, she could do calm.

She could—

The finger touched her neck again and she screeched, bouncing in the chair, lashing out her feet, her legs, snapping at the air with her teeth.

Manson cooed with surprise, the sound dissolving to a muted laugh. "Ah, my plans for you truly *are* perfect," he whispered directly into her ear from behind.

"Bite me," she snarled again, heart a cannon in her ears.

Fresh peals of laughter.

Glaring at the darkness, she drove her nails into her palm. "What kind of gutless coward ties up a girl?"

"I remember what you did to me when we first met," the hunter replied, stepping in front of her. He smiled, the room's murky light glinting off his teeth. And the blade in his hand. The same blade Kitt had sank into the side of his neck. "Tell me, what kind of gutless coward attacks an old man from behind?"

She glowered at him.

His smile widened. "Hello Amber. I've missed you. Have you missed me?"

"Where's Mick?" God, was her brother alive? Was Daku?

And what the hell was a dreamwalker?

...I need you to see where you... Daku's voice whispered through her head. A memory? No. It didn't feel like a memory. Memories had weight, substance. This was more ethereal, like wisps of sound and mist and...

Dream. Like a dream.

When had she dreamed of Daku? That was impossible. She hadn't slept since he'd appeared at the motel room to protect her. Since Kitt left her in his protection.

A cold lump rolled in her stomach and she sucked in a sharp breath.

If she was here, did that mean Daku was dead? That Mick was...

"Where's Mick?" she screamed up at Manson.

He narrowed his eyes, and took a step back. "If you're referring to the other...gentleman back at the motel, the large one, I don't remotely care. I left him there."

Biting back a sob, she scrunched her eyes shut. Was Mick still back at the motel? Was he dead? Alive?

God, please let him be alive and safe. Please let him be back at the motel. Unconscious. Conscious. Furious. Wondering what the hell had happened. Any of the above. Just as long as he's not here. Not—

"Please tell me you're not going to carry on with this racket until the dire wolf arrives?" Manson asked.

Sharp relief stabbed into her fear and she let out a sharp breath. Kitt was alive still. That was something.

"So that's your plan? Bait?" She forced an incredulous

tone into her voice. "You're using me as bait?" Huffing out a scoffing *pft*, she shook her head. "Lame."

"You're a feisty one, aren't you." Manson tapped his chin with a long, wrinkled finger. "I'm actually looking forward to changing you."

"And you're an old fart," she shot back. "I'm looking forward to— Wait, what? What do you mean, changing me?"

He wriggled his eyebrows, even as he shot a quick glance over his shoulder, and then pressed his index finger to his puckered lips. "Shh."

"Please don't do that," she complained. "You look like an idiot."

Rage flickered over his face and he swung his hand back, up behind his ear.

Amber flinched, ready for the strike.

And blinked when the sound of a throat clearing floated out of the darkness.

Tight, tingling heat rushed through her and she caught her breath, squinting into the dim room. Someone else was here.

Who?

Scowl twisting his face, Manson shot a look over her head. His eyes widened for a second and then, scowl turning to a sneer, he lowered his arm. "Excuse me for a moment, dear."

He hurried away. Gone.

Twisting on the chair as much as she could, she searched for any hint of the other person.

"Who's here with you?" she called.

Manson didn't answer, the room's heavy shadows hiding him once more.

Grinding her teeth, she tested the ropes again. Mick

had walked her through getting out of handcuffs once, but ropes?

Cold guilt washed over her. Mick. He'd hugged her as the motel door exploded in. Shielded her with his body.

Please please please be back at the motel, Mick. Talking to the cops. Talking to Kade, to Kitt. To Daku. Talking to anyone. Just please be alive. Please don't be dead. Please don't be—

"Amber?"

The low mutter, barely more than an exhaled breath, shattered the quiet.

Her heart slammed into her throat and she stiffened in the seat, staring into the darkness. "Mick?"

The whispered voice could belong to either of her brothers, but it had to be Mick in the dark with her. Ray was being guarded by an angel.

Mick had been in the motel room...

"Mick?" she repeated, as low as his. "Where—"

He hurried toward her from the shadows, checking over his shoulder.

"Mick!" She quivered on the chair, staring at him. "Are you okay? Are you hurt?"

"Shh," he hushed, squatting down beside her. "I need to get you out of this chair. We need to get out of here."

"Hurry." She twisted around, trying to watch him fight with the ropes. "Hurry. Manson could come back any second."

"Who?" Mick whispered, focus fixed on the knot.

"The creepy old guy," she said, turning back to the empty darkness in front of her. "His name's Manson. He's the owner of the bloody footprints you so wonderfully describe to me on the phone earlier this morning."

"Manson?"

She twisted back to him. "Are you laughing?"

He flicked her a quick look, and returned his attention back to the rope. "Don't worry about Manson," he muttered. "I think I've distracted the old fart. By the way, we're going to have a long talk about who you can and can't see when this is all finished."

"Not this again," she snapped. "Just hurry up. Is Daku here? Is he okay?"

If Daku wasn't okay, would Kitt know? Would anyone else at Guarded Souls contact him?

"Done," Mick breathed, lurching back to his feet at the second the ropes around her wrists fell free.

"Excellent." Relief gushed through her and she damn near threw herself from the seat, wrapping her arms around him. "Thank you thank you thank you."

She squeezed his solid girth, smacked a kiss on his stubbly cheek and, letting him go, bounced on her toes, shooting the space behind her, around her furtive glances. "We can argue later about who I'm seeing, I promise. Do you know if Daku is here?"

Mick straightened, studied her, and then slid his gaze over her shoulder. "No. But *Manson* and I have to have a little chat."

She gaped at him. "Are you kidding? We've got to get out of here. Call the cops, Mick. The *cop* cops. They can deal with him. I mean, do you even have your gun? Your badge? We have to go."

He turned to her, and tapped a finger to her lips. "Shh, sis. It's going to be okay."

"Listen to him, Amber," Manson stepped out of the shadows. "It truly is going to be okay. For me."

～

JAW CLENCHED, fists balled, Kitt ran a slow stare over the motel room.

Debris scattered the floor: wood from the destroyed door, glass from the shattered TV screen...

Amber had been in here when this happened. If he hadn't left her...

His gaze fell on the bed and his gut twisted.

On the floor beside it lay Amber's camouflage jacket, covered in plaster dust.

A red mist descended over his vision and a low growl rumbled deep in his chest, his skin itching with a million pin-pricks of searing heat.

Stop it.

Chest tight, gut churning, he forced his *croi* to subside, reigning in the shift.

An enraged dire wolf wouldn't save Amber. He needed to stay calm.

"I'm sorry, mate," Dak said, coming to stand beside him. "I let you down. I know that."

Kitt ground his teeth, stare sliding back to the bed. Her scent still hung on the air, delicate and clean—the soap from her recent shower, the smell that was distinctly hers, her fear...

"Did you get a look at the attacker, Dak?" Nim picked her way over the mess, frowning at it. "Is there anything I can use to locate—"

"She's in a large room somewhere," Dak said. "Looks like an abandoned cold-storage warehouse. I could only slip into her mind for a split second. Her dream wasn't strong—more a state of unconsciousness than anything else—but I got her to wake up and hung in her dream long enough while she was in the hypnagogia state to see—"

Kitt spun around, grabbed Daku's shirt front and hauled him off the floor. *"You were meant to protect her."*

"Kitt!" Nim snapped. "Stop it."

"It's all good, Nim," Dak murmured, black eyes holding Kitt's. "Let him."

Kitt snarled into his face, inner wolf coiling, flexing... "I entrusted you to protect her."

Daku nodded. That was it. Didn't fight back. Didn't thrash as Kitt drew him closer, feet dangling off the floor. "You did."

"So why *didn't* you?"

"Kitt," Nim moaned. "You need to calm down. You need to—"

"Let your anger feed you, mate." Dak's black eyes never wavered from Kitt's. "But don't let it rule you."

Kitt snarled, skin on fire.

Black light swirled in Dak's pupils. Swirled and spread, filling his entire eyes. Swirled and stormed and burned with ancient, timeless force. "I *will* help you find her, Kitt," he said, his voice low and calm and endless. "And I will make those that hurt her, took her, suffer in ways you can't even imagine, but you've gotta put me down first."

Kitt stared into his eyes. His *wolf* stared into his eyes. And with a slow, ragged breath placed Dak's feet back on the floor.

Outside, the wail of a distant siren grew louder.

"I think the cops are finally here," Nim muttered, shaking her head. "And we've achieved squat."

"Can you get anything?" Kitt's gut churned again. "Sense anything?" He scanned the room, head buzzing. No Amber. No Mick.

Had whoever attacked taken her brother as well? Why?

She shook her head again. "Not here. But I know the practitioner's signature now."

"Their what?"

"Every magic user has a unique substance they leave in every spell cast," Dak said, stepping carefully over broken bits of door as he headed deeper into the room.

"What Dak said." Nim nodded. "How do you know that, Dak?"

Without answering, Dak bent at the waist and picked Amber's jacket up from the floor.

Kitt sucked in a steadying breath. Outside the siren wailed louder. Closer.

Wordlessly, Dak crossed back to where he stood and handed it to him, dark eyes still entirely black. "We'll find her. And when the person who took her sleeps..."

"They're never going to *sleep* again," Kitt growled, turning and striding from the room. "I'll make sure of that."

The gasps of those outside—the other guests of the motel, and the gawkers drawn to chaos—scraped at his control.

He ignored them. Ignored everything.

Lifting Amber's jacket to his face, he closed his eyes and breathed in deeply.

Where was she?

"Kitt!" Nim's shout slammed into him from behind. "Kitt, I've found..." She ran out of the room, ignoring the fresh gasps from the onlookers, and grabbed Kitt's arm. "Is this hers? It was under a piece of door. I only found it because it started buzzing."

She shoved a phone—covered in plaster dust, its screen shattered—at him.

Hand shaking, he took it. Woke it up with a tap of his

thumb. A drawing of a dire wolf filled the cracked screen and he let out a low growl. He knew that image. Had traced its identical twin with his tongue on Amber's skin.

And on top of the image was a text message alert.

Unknown number, but unmistakable message: *Want her, wolf? Come get her. Alone.*

8

The phone vibrated in his hand as another message flashed up on the screen.

No, not a message. A shared location.

Kitt stared at it. Branded the location into his mind.

"Coming for you, fucker," he muttered, slipping Amber's phone into the hip pocket of his sweatpants, his flesh igniting in a wave of prickling heat as an image of the *Monstrum Venator* flashed through his head.

"You know it's a trap, right?" Worry swam in Nim's eyes.

"Take my bike." Dak tossed a set of keys at him.

Kitt snatched them out of the air and, with another growl, climbed onto Dak's Ducati and started the engine.

The siren's cut the air. The onlookers fell back, darting looks from Kitt, to Nim, to the approaching cops, to Daku, smartphones held up, recording it all.

"Of course it's a fucking trap." He smiled at Nim, his wolf baying deep within, ready, eager, impatient. "And I'm more than happy to spring it."

"I'm coming with you," Nim burst out, hurrying toward him. "I can help with the—"

He put the bike in gear and roared off.

Thanks to Guarded Souls work, Dak and Nim had more than enough experience with dealing with the cops. Nim could charm her way out of anything, and Dak...did what Dak did.

Kitt didn't worry about them. Here.

He *would* worry about them if they came with him to the confront the *Monstrum Venator*, and that wouldn't do. The only person he could worry about was Amber.

Jaw clenched, he shot through the streets, uncaring of posted speed limits, traffic signals and signs.

The Ducati purred like a beast beneath him. The wind lashed at his hair, whipped at the T-shirt Nim had bought him.

Gripping the handlebars, throttling up and down through the gears, he locked his stare on the road, slowing down only to avoid causing and accident and to preserve someone else's life. His skin prickled, every fiber in his being thrumming with the need to shift.

Not yet.

Not yet.

The *Monstrum Venator* had taken him by surprise the last time he'd hunted him, hadn't faced off with a dire wolf in full rage.

The bastard wasn't going to be so fortunate this time.

Trap or not, Kitt was finishing this.

The hunter wanted a dire wolf? He'd get a dire wolf.

Each turn taken, each block traveled, his *croi* burned hotter. More potent. Until, pulling to a halt a few yards from the location on Amber's phone, Kitt barely controlled it.

Dismounting the bike, he studied the grey, derelict

building situated far back from the empty road behind a tall fence topped with razor-wire.

His wolf pushed at his tenuous restraint.

Pulling a deep breath, he tasted the air.

And let out a low growl.

There. Faint. So faint it almost wasn't there. Amber's scent.

And with it, her brother's.

And the hunter's.

And...fear.

Whose?

The red mist returned. The air burned in his lungs.

His body thrummed.

Trap, Nim's voice whispered in his head.

"Trap," he muttered, rolling his shoulders.

Eyes narrowing, he pulled another deeper breath, and scanned the building's perimeter.

Any number of spots could be used to gain access, all obvious. All easy to reach.

Too obvious. Any number could be being watched.

"Trap," he muttered again.

Releasing his breath, he narrowed his focus down onto the darkening shadows climbing up the building's walls.

Shadows deep enough to lose sight of what they covered.

For a human...

There.

"Okay." He rolled his shoulders again and, checking the sun—sitting low in the western sky, fat and blinding-yellow—moved.

Fast.

The need to shift surged through him, but he resisted.

Until he saw Amber, until he knew she was safe, alive, he needed to keep control, however tenuous.

If she wasn't...

His *croi* flared hot, a wave of transformative force burning every molecule in his body.

No. Control it.

The glaring sun at his back, he vaulted over the fence, ran to the side of the building with inhuman speed and, tapping into his wolf's raw power, leaped up onto the small awning leaning at a precarious angle over what was once an entryway but was now a boarded up wall, covered in graffiti.

Unless someone was watching this very spot, or had motion detectors in place, it was unlikely he'd been seen.

Feet quiet, he moved over the to far edge of the rusted-iron roofed awning, calculated the distance to the broken window above it, and leaped.

Shards of glass sank into his fingers as he grabbed at the window sill.

He bit back a hiss, lifted his body upward, and—with a scan of the murky interior—climbed through the opening.

The stench of old decay, blood and metal bit into his senses. Death hung heavy in the air. What had this place once been?

Doesn't matter. All that matters is Amber.

Preparing himself for the impact, he dropped to the floor some twenty-feet below.

Somewhere deep in the bowels of the building, voices rumbled, the sounds low and agitated.

Crouching close to the ground, ready to throw himself forward, ready to shift if he needed, he strained to hear what was being said.

Nope. Too faint. Too soft. Whoever was arguing, he couldn't make out their words.

A thin ribbon of unease threaded through his rage. A building this size, he should be able to hear...

His wolf let out an agitated yip. *Focus. Find Amber.*

Dragging in another rot-tainted breath, he sought out her scent.

There.

Maybe?

To the right.

He squinted into the darkness, trying to discern the shapes lurking in the thin, filtered beams of pre-dusk penetrating the building's filthy skylight.

Another ribbon of disquiet unfurled through him.

Something wasn't right.

It's what Nim said. It's a trap.

He ground his teeth. No, that wasn't it.

He couldn't see as well as he normally could. Couldn't hear. His heightened non-human senses felt dampened. As if smothered.

His wolf stirred, restless. Eager for release. Hungry for blood. And yet...

Drawing motionless, he let the animal's existence seep into his own, releasing a little of his strangling grip, ready for the prickling heat that proceeded the transformation into wolf form.

Nothing.

A cold line traced up his spine. His scalp crawled.

Nothing.

The ability to shift. It wasn't there. It was gone.

Again.

His gut clenched, and he ground his teeth, furious.

Confused.

What the fuck? Why couldn't he shift? He was healed. Why couldn't he—

White light destroyed the darkness. Flooded the large room.

Hissing, he threw up his hand to shield his eyes. Eyes that took forever to adjust to the sudden change in light.

"Look who's finally here?" The *Monstrum Venator's* shout bounced around the glaring space, elation dancing through the words. "You snuck right on in without me knowing. Very clever of you."

Pulse pounding, adrenaline surging through him, Kitt squinted into the harsh light. Where was the asshole? He couldn't attack him until he pinpointed where he—

Kitt's blood ran to ice. His breath choked him.

Walking toward him, hand locked around Amber's elbow, thick dagger pointed to the side of her throat, the hunter smiled at him.

"Amber," Kitt burst out, taking a step.

"Uh-uh." The hunter twisted his wrist, turning the glistening tip of the blade against her skin. "Do you really want me to kill this feisty little monster fucker?"

"I *really* don't like this guy, Kitt," Amber complained, and then winced as the hunter pressed the knife harder to her neck.

Kitt stared at her. Impotent once more, his wolf snarled. Fought against the barrier once again imprisoning it in human form. "He's not my favorite person either, Am."

MANSON'S GRIP on Amber's arm turned painful. She tugged against him, trying not to obsess about the freaking knife jabbed into her neck.

"You two make an adorable couple." He sniggered, the smug sound making her want to break his old man's teeth. She shot him a sideways look. Were they false?

He dropped her a sly wink and her stomach lurched. "Shame I'm going to kill...well, both of you," he said.

"What?" she snapped.

"I will fucking tear you apart, hunter," Kitt growled.

"No." Manson shook his head, driving the tip of his dagger harder into her skin. How soon before her epidermal layer broke and the steel penetrated her flesh? "I will gut you with this very blade, and while you're bleeding out on the filthy floor—it's not very clean, is it—I will perform a wonderful little procedure that will transform your bitch here into a vampire and then I will hunt her, and kill her and add her to my kill count."

Amber jerked her stare back to the hunter. "I'm sorry, what?"

Another wink. "Don't worry. It won't hurt. The procedure, I mean. When I kill you *that's* going to hurt. A lot.."

"Fuck this," she muttered. Ah, crap this was going to hurt.

Clenching her teeth, she swung her fist around in the fastest haymaker Mick had ever taught her and smashed her fist into Manson's windpipe.

The tip of the blade pierced her skin, sliced it as she jerked around, and then it was gone. Slapping her hand to her neck, warm liquid oozing through her fingers, she reeled back, locked her sights on Manson—now staggering backward, eyes bulging—and smashed her bare foot into his gut.

Just as Kitt threw himself forward.

He slammed into the old man. Drove him to the floor.

Manson cried out, lashing the blade at Kitt. Slicing at his biceps, his shoulder.

Kitt roared, the sound ripped with pain and, fisting his hands in Manson's shirt, hauled him up off the floor and smashed him back down.

The solid clunk of Manson's skull smacking against the concrete reverberated through Amber.

Hand still pressed to her throat, palm and fingers growing wetter with blood, she staggered forward. Excruciating pain radiated out from the gash in her neck. Her vision blurred. What the hell was on that blade?

Where the hell was Mick?

He'd been in the small partitioned room with her and Manson before Kitt appeared. Manson had handcuffed him to one of the metal chairs, warning him not to do anything stupid, when Mick had calming informed him he'd seen someone dropping through a window out on the main floor.

Manson had grabbed her arm, and pointed his blade at Mick. "Don't move. We've got unfinished business."

And then he'd dragged her out of the small room, and she'd seen Kitt, and Kitt had seen her, and all hell broke loose and holy crap, where was Mick?

Another solid clunk vibrated through the floor, the sound accompanied by Manson's wails and Kitt's growls.

She swung her gaze over to them, blinking at the sweat in her eyes. The room swam, the burning in her neck growing hotter.

"Kitt..." she called, although it came out a slur. "I think...the knife's poisoned..."

He didn't respond.

Too busy dealing with Manson.

She let out a grunt, staggering sideways. Good.

"Go get 'im, Kitt," she shouted. Or maybe she mumbled. "Let him have it."

Where was Mick?

"Mick?" she yelled, turning around on the spot. "Mick?"

The guy knew how to get out of handcuffs. He should be here by now.

Fuzzy gaze sliding onto the little side room, she swallowed.

"Mick?" she called. While Kitt was dealing with the Manson, with the hunter, with Manson, she'd save Mick. She'd save her brother. Maybe then he'd stop treating her like a little kid.

Blood continuing to seep through her fingers, she peered at the partitioned area. "Maybe there's a band-aid in there?" she mumbled. "Whoa, my head feels doozy."

Behind her, Manson screamed. The sound of steel clattering against concrete scraped at her senses, and she swung back around, peering through the foggy haze.

Knife. Manson had lost his knife.

"I'll get it," she shouted—nope, yelled. Nope...called. Was she talking? Her throat felt thick. Dry. "I'll get..."

She lurched forward, looking for the knife. If *she* had the knife, Manson didn't. Then it'd be a fair fight.

"Going to kill—" Manson wailed, a second before another solid, meaty thud reverberated through the room, followed by a wet gurgle.

And then silence.

No not, silence.

Breathing. Harsh, ragged breathing.

"Am..."

Lifting her head, she found Kitt rising to his feet.

He swayed. No. She swayed. They both swayed? Or did the world sway? Who was swaying the world?

"Kitt," she whispered. "I think the knife is pois..."

She staggered sideways, vision blurring again.

"Amber," Kitt roared, running toward her.

"Stop right there, freak," Ray snarled.

Amber blinked. Ray?

Turning to the voice, she let out a relieved groan. Not Ray. Mick.

He strode out of the partition, the handcuffs dangling from one wrist and clinking against his leg, raising his other hand to point it at Kitt.

Amber frowned, rubbed at her eyes, and shook her head. "Mick, put the gun down."

Oh crap, she didn't feel good.

Mick shook his head, bearing down on her. "Shut up, Amber."

She glared at him. "Don't tell me to shut up."

Her neck burned. She mashed her palm to it some more. "I need some ice," she mumbled. "And a Band-aid."

"It's okay, Mick," Kitt said behind her, guarded tension in his voice. "It's not what it looks like. Trust me, I can explain, but you need to put the gun down."

Mick laughed, the sound as cold as his snarl. "I know *exactly* what it is. You're the one completely clueless to the situation. And you're not going anywhere near my little sister, again."

"You moron, I *love* your little sister," Kitt growled.

Mouth falling open, she gaped at him. "You what?"

He loves you?

Gaze flicking to her, Kitt lifted his shoulder in a small shrug, a smile tugging at his lips. "I love you."

She swallowed. Blinked. Frowned.

He loves you?

"Sorry," he said, voice husky. "And you're more than welcome to laugh at me and roll your eyes and tell me I'm insane and be angry at me...because I know it's too soon, but hopefully...you might one day feel the same. Or at least still like me enough to go for coffee with me again."

She blinked again, and let out a shaky breath. "You idiot. Of course I—"

"Shut the fuck up!" Mick screamed. "Amber, get out of the road. I have to take care of this monster."

Turning back to his brother, Amber shook her head. The burn was going away, but whoa, did her neck feel numb. And her lips. And her arm. "Stop it."

"Just put the gun down, Mick," Kitt said again, closer behind her.

"Don't take another step, freak," Mick ordered. "Amber, get behind me."

Amber shook her head again. "No. Listen to me."

"*Get behind me,*" Mick roared.

"Enough," Kitt growled back.

She heard him move. Heard his feet on the concrete floor.

And then the air shattered as Mick pulled the trigger.

"No," she screamed, spinning around.

Kitt stumbled backward, blood spurting from his shoulder, eyes burning gold.

She ran for him, and snapped to a halt, joints jolting, when Mick grabbed her upper arm in a steel grip. "I *said* get behind me, Amber."

"You've got it all wrong, you idiot." She clawed at his fingers, stare fixed on Kitt.

Kitt lurched to a halt, shoulders hunched, hand

rammed to the bullet hole in his shoulder. His breath burst from him in choppy pants. His nostrils flared.

"You've got it wrong," she cried again, swinging back to Mick. "He's not the bad guy."

Mick's jaw bunched. "I can't believe you..." His Adam's apple jerked up and down his throat, his stare—and his gun—locked on Kitt. "Tell me you didn't fuck him, sis? Please?"

"Oh my God, Mick." She pulled at his grip on her arm again, dug at his brutal fingers. "Enough already."

Blood trickled down over her collarbone. Its metallic twang filled her breath. "Stop it, so you can take us both to a hospit—"

"This monster's not going to a hospital, Amber." Mick slid her a glance, and her stomach rolled at the icy hate in his eyes.

"He's not a monster." She shook her head. Yeah, she seriously did not feel well. "He's—"

"A kill," Kitt said, the words low and calm, glowing eyes locked on Mick. "The end result of a hunt gone well. Am I right?"

Mick sucked in a slow breath, and released it on a slower laugh. "And finally, he gets it."

"Gets..." Amber blinked. "Gets what?"

Mick didn't answer, his focus turning back to Kitt.

"Gets what?" she repeated, frowning at Kitt.

He stood a little straighter, sweat beading on his forehead, eyes human again, blood leaking from the hole in his shoulder. "Do you want to tell her, Mick? Or will I?"

"Mick?" Lips tingling, blood cracking on her skin, she frowned at her brother. "What? Tell me what?"

"The old bastard rubbed my nose in every kill he made, y'know," Mick glared at Kitt. "Every one. When I found out he'd caught—and then *lost*—a dire wolf..." He grunted. "Of course I was going to make my move."

"Are you..." She swallowed. "Oh my God, Mick. Are you a..."

She couldn't say it. The words refused to form on her lips. From the blade's poison? Or because it wasn't true. It couldn't be.

"*Monstrum Venator*, sis." He bestowed a smile on her. Pride oozed from him. And arrogance. "Yes, I am. Have been since our parents died."

"What?" How many more times could she say that word today?

His smile turned into a twisted slash and he narrowed his eyes on Kitt. "They were killed by one of *his* kind, you know. A shifter."

"What?" There it was again. Did it have any meaning anymore? "I don't—"

"Bear shifter," he snarled.

"No. They died in a car accident. For Pete's sake, *you* were in the car with them. You were there. You were lucky to survive. Why are you lying about this?"

He barked out a cold laugh, never tearing his stare from Kitt. "The car rolled after slamming into a bear, sis. The bear was a shifter. It turned into a human just as Dad hit it. I saw it. I saw *him*."

Her stomach clenched. The world swam. "How do you... I don't... Does Ray know?"

Another short laugh. "Ray knows shit." He flicked her a sneer. "Ray saved this fucking shifter freak's life. Golden-boy Ray probably would have tried to save the bear shifter's life as well."

"I don't think Ray knows what I am, Am," Kitt murmured.

Mick's fingers dug deeper into Amber's arm, eyes narrowing again. "And he never will." He chuckled. "It's not like he's ever going to see you again, is he."

"Stop it, Mick." Amber shoved at him with her free hand. He grunted. "Stop it."

"Don't you get it, sis." He shook her arm, still staring at Kitt, gun leveled straight at him. "His kind? Monsters? They are a blight. They need to be eradicated. They're dangerous to people. They kill us and eat us and hunt us."

"*He* doesn't." She shoved at him again. This time he didn't even grunt. "Kitt doesn't do any of those things. You have *no* idea what you're talking about. I've been watching him for weeks and he's *never* done anything like that. *He's* the one that was hunted. *He's* the one that was shot and shoved in a cage and almost died."

"It's okay, Am," Kitt murmured.

"It's *not* okay," she snapped, glaring at him. Blood oozed from his shoulder. Bloody welts crisscrossed his shoulders and arms from Manson's attacks. "He doesn't even know you!"

"He attacked me, Amber." Mick yanked her backward, shaking her arm. "Remember? If it wasn't for you he would've tried to kill me."

"You burst into our room!" she shot back. "Unannounced. Let your self in. Broke in!"

"He fucking turned into dire wolf and attacked me." Mick shook her arm again. "I was trying to save you. I knew K5 was coming. I knew what he was planning to do to you. And then your wolf over there fucked off and left you and K arrived and I had to change my plans. Had to lull K into a false sense of security."

"K?"

Cold contempt flared in Mick's eyes and he threw a

quick nod in the direction of the motionless hunter on the floor. "My fellow *Monstrum Venator*."

"So you used your sister as bait."

Kitt's calm statement twisted a cold knot in Amber's stomach. She looked at him, her heart thumping faster at the anger burning in his golden eyes.

"Of course I used Amber as bait." Mick sneered. "K bragged about how you wouldn't be able to shift when you were near him. Something about some kind of proximity magic in the bullet he shot you with. I admit, killing you in your human form wasn't what I'd planned, it won't be anywhere near as satisfying, but as long as I kill you..." He grinned. "You did exactly what I wanted. *You* killed the old bastard. Not me. A guild member can't kill a guild member, but K5 deserved to die. He used magic after all. So *you*, freak," he jiggled his gun a little, its aim never moving from Kitt's chest, "tidied that mess up for me. Thank you by the way. I'm grateful. Not enough to let you live, mind. Killing the last dire wolf in existence." He let out a mock shiver. "It's going to be better than sex."

"You're welcome," Kitt murmured.

Amber frowned, staring at him.

The blood had stopped flowing from his wounds. In fact, didn't he have more knife cuts on his arm a moment ago? Didn't he...

"Now, with the old fart gone," Mick said, "I'll be one of the best *Monstrum Venator* in the U.S. And once *I* kill you, once the last dire wolf shifter in existence is gone..." He chuckled with a shrug, grip on Amber's arm turning to a pincer. "I'll be the best. Then I think I'll turn my attention to hunting a dreamwalker. Never done that before. They're always so hard to detect. Almost mythological. But you actually hand-delivered one to me. I would have killed him back at the motel, but unfortunately I had to follow K. Couldn't let him get away with my sister. Just like I'll never let a monster like you be with my sister a—"

"Enough," Kitt growled. Eyes glowing gold, shoulders hunching, he took a step forward.

Amber's chest tightened. Her breath caught in her throat.

Not a single wound marred his flesh. The bullet hole, the slashes from Manson's knife...all gone.

How had Mick not noticed that?

Another guttural growl tore the air. No longer human. Almost...

Wolf. He's about to shift. The proximity magic isn't working anymore. He's about to shift.

Mick's fingers clamped her arm tighter. "Wait. Are you..." He hurried back a step, dragging her with him. "No, you can't. The old bastard said you can't."

"The old bastard's dead." Amber's blood roared in her ears. Hope rushed through her. "Maybe the magic doesn't—"

Mick fired his gun.

"No," she screamed, twisting back to Kitt just as he lunged forward.

And shifted form.

She yelped, pulling at Mick's hold, heels slipping on the filthy floor as she tried to scramble backward. Tried to break Mick's grip.

Tried to grab his wrist and pull him with her.

"*Kitt, don't,*" she screamed.

Don't what? Save her? Kill her brother? Be a dire wolf?

"Don't," she screamed again, as Mick squeezed off another round.

If the bullet hit Kitt, he didn't react. Or slow.

The massive dire wolf charged at them, glowing golden eyes locked on Mick, teeth bared, hackles raised.

Mick fired again, yanking on her wrist.

Throwing her into Kitt's path.

The dire wolf snarled, and leaped over her, just as— completely out of balance—she hit the ground.

Pain detonated in her knees, her elbow, her shoulder. Her teeth snapped shut, blood filling her mouth as she bit the side of her tongue.

She cried out, scrambling back up to her feet, head swimming, as Mick screamed behind her.

Another shot fired.

She spun around, stomach dropping as the dire wolf slammed into her brother, driving him to the floor, his gun skidding across the concrete.

"Kitt," she shouted. "Stop."

Kitt growled, and—fangs bared—pinned Mick to the floor.

Mick thrashed and punched at Kitt's massive head. Bucked beneath him.

Kitt didn't move. Just drew his muzzle closer to Mick's face, his deep growl vibrating through Amber's very soul.

"Please," she whispered, one hand out as she inched closer to the dire wolf's side. "Don't."

"Get off me," Mick wailed, bucking under Kitt's immovable weight.

The wolf snarled again, muzzle almost at Mick's face.

One snap of his powerful jaw, and Mick would be dead.

"Please," Amber whispered, heart racing, breath strangling her. She brushed her fingertips on Kitt's side. Willed him to look at her.

Growl growing louder, deeper, fangs glistening, the dire wolf pressed the end of his muzzle to Mick's cheek.

"Please." She curled her fingers gently in Kitt's thick fur. "He's my brother."

The growl died away.

Trapped, panting, Mick stared at Kitt. "I'm sorry," he rasped. "I'm sorry."

Amber took a step closer, the powerful beat of Kitt's heart thumping through his side into her palm. "Please," she murmured.

The wolf's head lifted and, with a shimmer of light and air and reality, Kitt straightened to his feet and stepped backward.

A ragged laugh fell from her.

Kitt's gaze found hers, his eyes human and beautiful and torment. "Am...I..."

She smiled. "I love—"

"No." Mick lunged at Kitt, a short, ugly dagger in his hand.

Kitt dropped into a crouch.

Just as Amber shoulder-slammed Mick, sending him sprawling to the ground.

"Enough," she snapped, destroying the distance between them. "Enough." She grabbed Mick's shirtfront, yanked him up as high as she could, and smashed her fist into his nose. "Enough."

Mick's eyes rolled back into his head and, heavy and limp, he dropped back to the floor. Thud.

Amber jabbed a finger at his motionless form. "You taught me how to do that, brother. Karma's a bitch, isn't it."

Mick didn't reply. His nose whistled, his shallow breath streaming through the thin trickle of blood seeping from his right nostril.

"Bet Alan Grant never did that," she muttered, straightening. She turned to Kitt, flexing and curling her fingers. "Oh my God, that hurt my hand."

He laughed, and leaped forward as she stumbled sideways, the world swimming into a sickening blur.

"Oh boy," she mumbled, as his arm whipped around her back. "I really don't feel..."

Every went black.

BRIGHT LIGHT ASSAULTED HER EYELIDS.

Grimacing against the intrusion, she forced her eyes open, and shoved herself up onto her elbows.

"Did you know we have the same blood type?" Mick said to her left.

She jerked around to face him, groaning at the unfamiliar tug and pull on her neck. What?

Ray raised his eyebrows at her.

Ray. Not Mick.

"Where am I?" She frowned again, casting her surroundings a squinted look as she pressed her fingers to the bandage taped to the side of her neck where Manson's knife had pierced and slashed her skin.

Hospital?

"Hospital," Ray answered. "You lost a lot of blood, sis. Almost too much. If Kitt hadn't got you here—"

"Kitt," she burst out, snapping up straighter, swinging her stare around the small room. "Where is he?"

The room was devoid of Kitt, its single armchair empty, its space bereft of his massive size.

Mouth dry, throat thick, she looked back at Ray. "Where..."

His own frown creasing his forehead, Ray shook his head.

A tight breath fell from her and she slumped back onto the narrow bed. "Well, that sucks."

"He said you didn't need the danger of his life," Ray offered, his voice gentle. "Given you're here with a knife wound to the neck, recovering from blood poisoning, with a fractured shoulder and three broken bones in your right hand, I'm inclined to agree with him. What the hell happened?"

She stared blankly at the room's ceiling, head roaring. "How long have I been out for?"

"Almost a week."

Her stomach clenched. A hot lump filled her throat.

He'd left her. Again.

Bastard.

"Where's Mick?" she asked, the words scratchy.

Ray cleared his throat. "Mick's in hospital. You broke his nose. Fragments of cartilage have been pushed up near his brain. He's not permanently damaged, but he's in a lot of pain."

"Good," she muttered, closing her eyes.

Kitt was gone. He'd left her.

An emptiness crept through her, as if a bleak winter was seeping into her bones, her soul.

"What happened, sis?" Ray took her hand—the non-broken one—a let out a confused grunt. "All Kitt would tell me is Mick tried to kill him and you stopped him. Why would he do that?"

Why indeed?

"What did Mick tell you?" The emptiness crawled over her heart. Her brother... How could Mick...

Ray cleared his throat again. "He's under police guard. I can't see him."

She opened her eyes and frowned. "Do the cops think his life is in danger?"

Would Kitt come after him? After everything that happened, she wouldn't blame him, but would he? Would Daku? Mick had threatened to hunt him. Had Kitt told the dreamwalker?

A shaky sigh escaped Ray and he shook his head. "Apparently Mick's been killing people, Amber. He owns a derelict cold storage warehouse out in the warehouse district, although it only looks derelict from the road. It's full of corpses, sis. In various states of decay. Male, female, little kids... All stacked up in one of the freezers there. And there's a cache of weapons there—guns, knives, cross-bows. Shit, it's like a big-game hunter went insane. Or a dooms-day prepper. And Mick's fingerprints are over all of them. The weapons, the door to freezer, just about every-thing inside." A raw sound fell from and he shook his head. "For a forensic cop, he sucked at cleaning up his tracks."

Closing her eyes again, Amber bit at the inside of her mouth.

She wasn't going to cry. Screw that.

"Alan Grant wouldn't cry," she muttered. "Or Indiana Jones."

Ray squeezed her hand. "You've got to tell me what happened. I spoke to the doctor. They don't know what the poison was in your blood. Nor why it left your system. They can't explain it, but they've never encountered anything like it. The cops have questions. The doctor has questions. *I* have questions. Just what the hell is going on?"

Letting out a wobbly laugh, she opened her eyes and smiled up at him. "I fell in love."

He blinked.

She closed her eyes again. "I think I need to sleep."

"You are the most exasperating sister on the planet," Ray mumbled, dropping a soft kiss on her forehead. "And I love you and I'm so glad your safe."

She smiled.

And fell backward into the nothingness of sleep.

...THE SOFT SCRATCH of bristles over dirt played with her senses. She gently moved her hand, twisted her wrist, left to right, exposing the fossilized bone with each stroke of the small brush.

Ahh, there...the metatarsal of a mature canis dirus. *The best specimen she'd ever found. Lifting her head, she smiled at the man beside her, ready to share her discovery. And then sighed. That's right, Kitt wasn't there. She was alone at the dig.*

Alone.

She returned to the fossil, brushing at it. Grain by grain, exposing it to her gaze. To the world. Revealing it for everyone to see.

Her hand paused and she frowned. She didn't want to expose it. She didn't want everyone knowing about it. It was special and amazing and mystical and the world would only fear it. She didn't want to share it. She only wanted...

Kitt.

Kitt.

She lifted her head and frowned at the empty dig.

And smiled at the man walking towards her through the trees.

I've kicked him in the arse for you, Amber. Daku smiled, stopping to stand a little away from her, dark eyes endless and swirling and hypnotic. Gave him a damn good ear-bashing. He's coming. He's on his way.

I'm here, Am, *a low, deep rumble sounded around the dig.* I'm...

An idiot, *she murmured, opening her eyes...*

...TO SCOWL UP AT KITT.

Worry ate up his face. The muted light of the hospital room seemed to make his golden eyes glow. Or maybe it was the ancient magic of what he was.

He sucked in a shaky breath, and let it out again, taking her hand in his as he brushed a strand of hair from her forehead.

"Bout time you turned up," she whispered.

"You knew I was here?" he whispered back, brushing her forehead, her temple again.

She lifted her shoulder in a small shrug. "Daku told me you were coming. In my dream just now."

"Did he?"

She nodded. Once. Her neck still hurt.

"I'm sorry." He shook his head. "I thought I was doing the right thing for you. I thought I was protecting you, saving you."

"I don't need you to save me, Kitt." She lifted her bandaged hand and gave it a little jiggle. "I can do that myself, see? But if I'm not around, who's going to save you?"

His eyes glowed brighter. A low groan vibrated deep in his chest, became an even lower growl. "Did you know dire wolves mate for life?"

Lowering her hand, she arched an eyebrow. "Is this your way of proposing?"

He chuckled, dipping his head so his forehead kissed hers. "This is my way of saying this old canine is ready for you to teach him a new trick."

She lifted her bandaged hand again and brushed her gauze-wrapped knuckles against his jaw. "You realize paleontologists get off on really old things, right?"

His laugh rumbled through his body into hers. "When you get out of here, want to rub my belly?"

Snagging the front of his shirt with her other hand, she grinned up into his eyes and pulled his head down to hers. "Hell. Yeah."

EPILOGUE

Confused shock on his face, the cop jerked his hand to his gun in its holster.

Ray let out wry laugh, raising his hands, palms forward. "It's okay. I'm his twin. Identical twin. Can I see him?"

Frown taking the place of his stunned bewilderment, the cop shook his head. "Sorry. I can't let anyone in. Not even family."

Gut clenching, Ray nodded, dropping his hands. "I understand. Can I get him a message?"

The cop narrowed his eyes, hand never leaving his gun's grip. "Maybe you should talk to his lawyer? If he has one."

"It's a simple message," Ray said, the churning sensation in his stomach broiling into a choking storm. He flicked the closed door behind the cop a quick glance. Pictured Mick inside, handcuffed to the bed, face—so much like his own people could rarely tell them apart—swollen and bandaged.

Grunting, the cop removed his hand from his gun and

folded his arms over his broad chest. "Fine. Tell me what it is. I'll give it to him."

Returning his attention to the police officer, Ray swallowed. "Tell Mick I know what he did to Amber. Tell him, I hope he rots in hell."

The cop sucked in a swift breath, and dipped his head in a single nod.

Ray turned and walked away from his twin's room.

A *Monstrum Venator's* work was never done.

EPILOGUE II

Pulling in a slow breath, the lights of his living room dimmed, the soft night breeze wafting through the window, Dak crossed his legs, rested his wrists on his bent knees and closed his eyes.

Waiting this long to fulfil his promise to Kitt hadn't been easy, but *this* walk was different. It needed the right moment. The right time.

The breeze fanned his face, lifted his hair from his forehead. Streamed over his bare chest, flowed around his bare arms, his bare legs. The sounds of the night outside faded, replaced by the steady beat of his heart and the ancient whispers of the universe.

He let out his held breath, sinking into himself. Sinking into the realm of the impossible.

Falling into the swirling, infinite vastness. Falling into the river where it all came from, the spring of thought and dreams and life. Stepping into the Dreamtime. Stepping into someone's dream. Walking into...

...the forest.

Fuck, the freak's got away. *Mick stopped, spun around,*

scanning the looming underbrush, the towering redwoods. The dire wolf was here somewhere. He'd find it. Gut it. Skin it. Slowly. Make it suffer for touching Amber. Make it bleed and howl and beg for release, beg for death.

Coming for you, freak. Mick's voice echoed around the forest, and he smiled. Going to fucking kill...

Dak stepped up behind him. Look over there, he whispered into Mick's ear. See him?

Mick snapped his head to the side, crossbow raised.

Waving a hand to the left, Dak conjured Kitt's image.

Mick shouted with joy and fired.

The crossbow bolt passed through Kitt's shape, just as Dak pressed his finger to the base of Mick's spine.

Mick screamed, arching back, blood gushing from his mouth.

Dak removed his finger and Mick staggered forward.

Once. Twice.

Lifting his palm to the endless black sky, Dak made Mick stand upright.

Look over there, he whispered into Mick's ear again. See him?

He waved his hand to the right, projecting Kitt's image.

Got you, Mick snarled, firing the crossbow again.

Kitt's form evaporated as the bolt sheared through it. As Dak flicked the back of Mick's neck.

Mick screeched, blood spurting from his nose.

Over there, Dak stated, pointing over Mick's shoulder.

Mick hefted up the crossbow, aimed it at Kitt, released the bolt. At the very second Kitt became Mick.

The bolt slammed into Mick's chest and he cried out, reaching for himself...

Dak tsked behind the pierced Mick, shook his head and lifted his palm again.

Mick straightened, trembling.

I don't... *Mick whimpered, crossbow shaking in his hands.* I don't like this...

Stab him, *Dak whispered, throwing Kitt's image at Mick.*

Mick gibbered and flailed and swung the knife now in his hand at the dire wolf, each slash opening his own skin, drenching him in blood.

No... *Mick sobbed, shaking his head, stumbling backward, as the dire wolf faded to mist.* No...wake up, Mick. Wake...

Dak flicked his hand and the dire wolf leaped at Mick again. Slammed into him.

Pinned him to the ground.

Got you, *Mick whispered sneering down at himself.* Going to gut you, skin you, kill you for what you did to Amber.

Underneath himself, Mick thrashed and screamed and wailed and cried as the dream began to erode his sanity. As the images in his mind began to unravel the threads of his mind. Stop, stop, stop...

Smile slowly curling his lips, Dak settled down, cross-legged on the dream's cool grass and rubbed his hands together.

Okay, *he murmured to himself,* let's really make this fun...

THANK YOU

If you enjoyed **Amber's Heat**, follow Lexxie on Bookbub for pre-order, sales and new-release alerts. Sign-up for her newsletter, the Lexxicon to receive a free copy of her (erotic) paranormal short story, **The Cavern**, plus never miss out on exciting announcements and giveaways!

ABOUT LEXXIE COUPER

Lexxie writes fun-with-feels romances. She lives with a manic rescue dog, a self-absorbed rescue cat, a very patient husband not rescued from anything, and two strong-willed teenage daughters who will one day rule the world.

Lexxie lives by two simple rules – measure your success not by how much money you have, but by how often you laugh, and always try everything at least once. As a consequence, she's laughed her way through many an eyebrow raising adventure. You can find details of her writing at
www.LexxieCouper.com

COMING SOON

Elora's
DREAM

LEXXIE COUPER
INTERNATIONAL BEST-SELLING AUTHOR

ELORA'S DREAM

GUARDED SOULS, BOOK FOUR

Coming Soon in Print and Digital

She never dreams...until Dax enters her life. But can the
dreamwalker save her, or will her nightmares devour her?

ALSO BY LEXXIE COUPER

Fire Mates Series

Sera's Dragon
How to Love Your Dragon
Crouching Tigress, Sexy Dragon
Enter The Dragon
Dragon, Interrupted

Guarded Souls Series

Destiny's Knight
Hope's Wish
Amber's Heat

Dark Sentinel Series

Dark Destiny
Dark Embrace

Savage Australis Series

Savage Retribution
Savage Transformation